Janet Dailey
Americana

BOSS MAN FROM OGALLALA

Harlequin Books

TORONTO • NEW YORK • LONDON
AMSTERDAM • PARIS • SYDNEY • HAMBURG
STOCKHOLM • ATHENS • TOKYO • MILAN
MADRID • WARSAW • BUDAPEST • AUCKLAND

The state flower depicted on the cover of this book is goldenrod.

Janet Dailey Americana edition published July 1987
Second printing August 1988
Third printing August 1989
Fourth printing August 1990
Fifth printing October 1991
Sixth printing March 1992

ISBN 0-373-89877-0

Harlequin Presents edition published March 1976
Second printing September 1977
Third printing December 1978
Fourth printing June 1979

Original hardcover edition published in 1975
by Mills & Boon Limited

BOSS MAN FROM OGALLALA

CHAPTER ONE

"NO KISS FOR THE OLD MAN today, Casey love?" the weak voice asked from the hospital bed.

A determinedly happy smile curled the corners of her mouth upward as Casey Gilmore dodged the hanging ropes and weights that held her father's leg in traction. She brushed her lips lightly over his, noting the pallor under the mahogany tan of his skin. Not even the steady dose of painkillers had erased the reflection of pain in his brown eyes, only dulled their brilliance.

"Sorry to be so late, dad." The cheerful smile on her face didn't reach her troubled eyes as Casey glanced briefly at her mother seated in a chair next to the bed before she herself sat in the adjacent chair.

"We were just beginning to worry about you." Her mother studied her closely, her teasing voice showing the concern and apprehension that had become commonplace these last few days.

"I had lunch with Johnny before he went back to North Platte," Casey explained, keeping her voice purposely light so her father wouldn't know how disappointed she was with the results of that talk. She brushed her short-cropped brown hair away from her equally dark eyes in a nervous gesture, sensing that despite the lightness of their greetings, her parents had been having a serious discussion before her arrival. "I see you haven't started chasing the nurses yet," she jested to fill the silence.

"Not likely to, either," John Gilmore sighed. His dark hair, just beginning to become flecked with gray, moved restlessly on the white pillow. "Six weeks in this contraption!" His eyes looked at the ceiling in desperation even as he muttered what amounted to a curse. "Of all the times to get thrown by a horse, this wasn't one of them. How are things at the ranch, Casey?"

She had trouble meeting his earnest gaze. How glad she was that her mother had spent the last few days in Scottsbluff with her father so that she didn't know the latest crisis that had occurred. Her mother was horribly transparent about her feelings and couldn't have kept a thing from her husband no matter how hard she tried.

"Outside of everyone missing you terribly, everything's fine." Casey's fingers lay crossed in her lap; she refused to think about the broken water pump or the ten head of cattle missing from the Burnt Hollow pasture.

"You wouldn't be keeping anything from me, Casey?" he asked with his usual perception at reading her mind.

"You're a worrier! The most serious thing that's happened since your accident is that Injun threw a shoe," Casey grimaced. "And I wish he'd broken a leg so I could shoot him."

The weak chuckle at his tender-hearted daughter's vehement statement couldn't compare with his usual robust laughter. "I probably would have loaded the gun for you." His expression grew more serious as he glanced briefly at his wife, then back to Casey. "Fred Lawlor from the bank stopped in this morning after you and Johnny left," he said.

Not more problems, Casey groaned inwardly, knowing how precarious their position had become financially since the cattle market had taken such a nose dive. Her father's face told her that his oldest friend hadn't stopped merely in friendship.

"That was very kind of him," she commented aloud.

"Yes, yes, it was." John Gilmore moved uncomfortably in the bed. The white hospital gown looked unnatural covering his chest. "He made a suggestion that your mother and I have been talking over." Casey stiffened unconsciously. "He knows I'm going to be in traction for at least six weeks while this broken hip mends. And after that—well, I'm not a young man anymore. Even with the surgery that inserted the steel pin, it's going to take time for my creaky old bones to heal. In the meantime, the running of the ranch has pretty well been dumped in your lap."

"I can handle it, dad," Casey asserted quickly. "We already finished all the dipping, branding and vaccinating before you got hurt. Mark will be out of school soon and he can lend a hand, even if he is only fifteen. You'll be up and around to supervise the fall work." The sympathetic exchange of glances between her parents told Casey that her arguments weren't successful. "Sam's there, too. If I need extra help, you know Smitty will always come over. Dad, I am twenty-one. I know every inch of the ranch. I've lived there all my life."

"I'm not doubting your ability. I've never pulled any punches with you or your mother. You know how hard we were hurt last year between the late spring blizzard and the cattle prices. If it wasn't for the rising land values, I don't know if I could have got another loan from the bank. Fred Lawlor knows you pretty well. If it was his choice, he'd trust you to take care of things." He couldn't meet her eyes any longer as his gaze shifted to his right leg dangling in the air. "The bank suggested that we bring someone else in to run the ranch until I'm in a position to take over myself."

Casey's teeth bit hard into her lips to keep her pointed chin from trembling. Staring down at the creases in her western cut blue pants and the pointed toes of her beige dress boots, she inhaled deeply. "It's because I'm a female, isn't it? If Johnny were home it would be different, wouldn't it?"

"Don't be bitter, dear," her mother said quietly. "It's just the way things are."

"Women's Lib sure know what they're talking about." Casey attempted to laugh, but only a bitter sound came out as she rose from her chair and walked to the window, her face clouded over.

"If there was a chance that I could recuperate at home, they probably wouldn't have even considered it. You have to face facts, Casey," her father said, "you can't consider a two-hour drive one way as being close in an emergency."

"But you're the only boss man the Anchor Bar has ever had," Casey protested. "I don't know if I could take orders from anyone else but you. Can't you talk to Mr. Lawlor? Can't you persuade him to—"

"He knows a man from Ogallala," John Gilmore interrupted firmly, "who's extremely experienced and capable. I've already told him to get hold of him and send him out." A little more gently he added, "I'd like to know I can depend on you to help things run smoothly for him."

"Take it like a man, huh?" Casey didn't bother to hide her bitterness, knowing that she and her father were too close for him not to know it was there. Her chin jutted out determinedly as she turned from the window toward him. "You can depend on me, dad, but you knew that all along."

"I was pretty sure of it," he said smiling, "but I feel better now that I've heard you say it."

A nurse walked into the room carrying a tray. "It's that time again, Mr. Gilmore." She glanced at Casey and her mother with a silent request that they leave.

"I'll say goodbye now, dad." Casey walked over to kiss her father's cheek. "I want to get home before Mark does." She paused. "This man that's coming, when should I expect him?"

"Fred said he'd try to get him out there the first of the week."

Casey raised her eyebrows and then smiled. It gave her at the most five days to make sure everything was shipshape. "Mark and I will be down Sunday," she promised, giving him a thumbs-up sign as she followed her mother out the door.

Outside she paused with her mother, taking in the pinched lines around her mouth and the way her dress hung loosely around her waist. Casey had often admired her mother's devotion to her husband. Now she could see the toll that love had taken in the four days since the accident. The serene composure of Lucille Gilmore's delicate features faded as she turned to her daughter.

"You do understand, don't you, Casey, that your father was hardly in a position to argue with the bank?" she said.

"I can understand it without liking it."

"To be truthful, I'm glad," her mother sighed, her blue eyes glancing apologetically at Casey. "I didn't like you shouldering all that responsibility alone, not when things are so difficult."

"Everything's going to turn out fine, mom. You just worry about dad and leave the ranch and the new boss man to me to worry about."

"All these years I've been so concerned about you being such a tomboy in some ways. Now with Johnny working for the railway instead of taking over the ranch like your father and I had planned, I guess we can be glad you're the way you are. When this is all over and John is back home—" There was a catch in her voice.

Casey laughed with the same tight sound to her voice that her mother had. Neither one of them could discuss the subject most prominent on their minds, that of the man lying in the hospital room with a broken hip. Even Lucille Gilmore's inquiries about her youngest son, Mark, were asked with the thought that if it weren't for her husband's injuries, she would be home with him.

After exchanging parting kisses, Lucille promised, somewhat reluctantly, that she would be returning home with Casey and Mark when they came to the hospital on Sunday. Casey could tell that her mother was torn between her desire to be at her husband's side and to be with her children. She had learned that despite her mother's outward look of delicate womanhood she was an exceptionally strong woman inside. The subject had probably been discussed thoroughly with her father and the result had been decided. There was no need for Casey to try to dissuade her that it wasn't necessary. Both of her parents' minds would rest easier knowing that Lucille was at the ranch with their children.

As Casey left the hospital, she toyed with the idea of making a side trip to North Platte to meet with her older brother again, to renew her earlier pleas at lunch that he return to the ranch to help out in this new crisis. She had only to remember his forceful refusal to her suggestion. During his teens, John had tried to live up to his father's wishes that he learn ranching so that he could one day take over, but after he had finished school, he had enlisted in the armed forces. While overseas, he had written Casey telling her that he had decided not to go back to working for his father. His enlistment had ended in the late summer of last year and he had wasted no time in letting his parents know that he was taking a job with the Union Pacific Railroad in North Platte.

The disappointment had been a bitter pill for her parents, combined with all the setbacks they had suffered, but whatever they felt had been concealed. Casey could only guess at the pain he had felt when her father had sent his eldest son on to make his own future. She had secretly hoped that during her luncheon with her brother she would have been able to persuade him to return, even temporarily. Johnny had been sympathetic and ashamed when he refused.

"I made the break once," he had said. "I know

dad would never stand in my way. But don't you see how guilty I feel letting him down? I know how much he was counting on me. If I came back now, I'd be building his hopes up again. Let's face it, Casey, you think more of that ranch than I do."

But the following statement that he had made was the one that forestalled Casey from contacting him again about the news that someone was coming to take over control of the ranch.

"If things get too much for you, sis, you and dad can hire someone a lot more experienced than I am," Johnny had finished.

Her journey back to the ranch was made with a combination of anxiety and anger. The thought of her father confined to that hospital bed for six weeks when he was needed so badly at the ranch weighed as heavily as the rebellion that some stranger would be in charge of their future.

CHAPTER TWO

THREE MILES AFTER TURNING on the graveled road that led to the ranch lane, Casey saw a pickup truck just turning out of the Smith ranch. Both horns honked at the same time as Casey slowed her car to a halt. She rolled the window down and smiled her hello at the figure in faded denims and battered straw Stetson that hopped out of the cab of the truck.

"Just gettin' back from the hospital?" Smitty asked, lifting the hat from his head long enough to wipe the perspiration off his forehead as he leaned against the car.

Casey nodded, gazing up into the deeply tanned face, young and boyishly handsome with its eagerness for life. His eyes were a warm brown that had a perennial twinkle in them. His hair was a peculiar chocolate brown, growing long and thick to hang below his ears and mingle with his sideburns, long enough to be in style and short enough not to incur his father's wrath. Smitty, or more correctly, Don Smith, was the only child of Robert and Jo Smith, the Gilmores' nearest neighbors. Smitty was, at twenty-three, the same age as Johnny,

Casey's brother. Ever since Casey could remember she had been tagging after the two of them, until she was seventeen, then Smitty had suddenly taken an interest in her. Unlike Johnny, they both shared a love for ranch life, sports and animals.

"Dad's doing a lot better. He's still in a lot of pain, but you know him, he never complains," Casey smiled, her pride showing with the love for her father.

"We're driving down Sunday," Smitty said. "How's things at your place?"

"The water pump broke at the number ten well. Sam tried to fix it, but he's no good with motors. I was wondering—"

"If I'd come over and take a look at it," Smitty finished with a laugh. "Sure I will. My old man's given me a free hand to come over any time you need me. Were you able to talk Johnny into coming back?" Casey had confided in him the previous day that she was going to try.

"No." The deep sigh that accompanied her negative reply told him the futility of the attempt which he had already predicted. "That's not all either." Casey's hand clenched the steering wheel in a nervous, angry gesture. "Fred Lawlor from the bank is making arrangements for a man to come in and take over the ranch operations until dad is on his feet."

Smitty's eyebrows raised at the announcement while he exhaled a silent whistle. He had known

Casey too long not to know what her reaction to that news had been.

"They don't trust a woman," she added, her forehead knitting together in a bitter frown.

"My poor little independent Casey is going to have to take orders from some big boss man," Smitty teased. At her glowering stare, he reached out and let his fingers follow the gathering of freckles that bridged her nose before his finger ended up under her chin, which he lifted as he leaned inside the window and planted a firm kiss on her lips. "I'm glad. I never did want my girl tied down to a ranch twenty-four hours a day for the rest of the summer."

Casey knew she should have felt flattered by his pronouncement, but the idea of someone other than a Gilmore holding the reins of the Anchor Bar ranch was more than she could tolerate. Her sense of humor completely deserted her on that subject.

"How would you feel if someone came in and started bossing you around on your ranch?" she retorted. "You're not a woman, so it probably would never happen to you."

"Ah, come on, Casey, don't take it as a personal insult." He had heard her before when she got started on the subject of equality between the sexes. He had the feeling that she was about to step up to the podium again. "It's not going to be forever."

"I thought you'd understand," she accused.

"I do. It's just no good getting upset about something you can't change. Which reminds me, I was flying over the west pasture today. I think I saw those ten head of cattle you were missing mixed in with our own herd over there," he informed her.

"That means there's a fence down somewhere," Casey sighed, relieved that the cattle had been found and were not rustled as she had feared.

"I'll meet you out there tomorrow and we'll check it out," Smitty offered.

"Thanks. I want everything in perfect order when this... this man comes."

"Who is it?"

"Somebody from Ogallala," Casey shrugged. She had been too upset to get any details. "I'd better be going. I want to be home before Mark."

"The bus went by about a half hour ago." He tapped the car lightly with his hand as he moved back toward the pickup. "Say, we had a date for Saturday night. Is it still on?"

"I have to go into Scottsbluff with Mark. Why don't you just come over and we'll watch some TV or something?" Casey suggested, shifting the gears into reverse and backing on to the road as Smitty waved his agreement.

Two miles farther on the graveled road, Casey turned on to the lane leading back to the ranch house grounds. Her eyes instinctively studied the rolling hills, the sturdy prairie grass beginning to change from its spring green color to a straw-colored yellow, the darker green dots of yucca plants, and the colorful rusty-red hides of the Hereford cattle. The hills stretched out interminably from horizon to horizon, the skyline broken occasionally by towering windmills. Following the curving track around one deceptively larger hill, Casey saw the small valley open before her and the buildings that signified home nestled against the bottom of the north side so that the hills could shelter them from the blasts of the cold north wind.

Bounding out from under the wooden porch at the sound of the slowing car came a dog of such mixed parentage that he always proved a topic of conversation. His ears were erectly pointed; his coat was long and shaggy; his forehead was wide and his nose was long; and the bushy tail wagged happily. Everyone agreed there was a shepherd breed somewhere in his ancestry, but one look at the black and tan color led everyone to speculate whether he was mixed with a coyote or a German Shepherd or both. But Shep was a member of the family and had been since the day he wandered into their yard, a frightened, skinny puppy. He was no longer skinny as all ninety-five pounds of him launched himself at Casey, the most cherished member of his adopted family.

Mark appeared on the porch as Casey greeted the exuberant dog and gradually quieted him to a more controllable state. She smiled at the ungainly boy with his denim Levis that stopped above his ankles, betraying the way he had suddenly grown this spring. His crumpled shirt was unbuttoned, leaving his ribs to poke out of his tanned chest. Mark had the same sandy hair and blue eyes of their mother and promised to be as tall as their six-foot father. He was already eye level to Casey, who was five foot four inches tall.

"It's about time you got home," Mark grumbled in a voice that threatened to break into a squeak with each word. He more or less collapsed into one of the porch chairs and picked up a worn pair of boots sitting beside the door. "I'm starved. Can't we go into town tonight and have a pizza?"

"Are the chores done?" Casey asked, ignoring his never-ending plea for food.

"No, I just got home."

"Smitty said the bus went by his place a half hour ago, which means you've had time to finish those cookies Mrs. Barker sent over and the half gallon of milk in the refrigerator," Casey replied perceptively. "That should give you enough energy to do chores."

"I was hungry," he shrugged, pulling on his boots. "How's dad?"

"Better, I think."

"Do I have to go to school tomorrow? Can't you take me in to see him and write me an excuse?"

"Good heavens, Mark, tomorrow is Friday. One more day isn't going to hurt you. Besides, next

Wednesday is your last day before the summer holidays." She walked up the steps onto the porch. "Hurry up with the chores."

Mark was still grumbling as he clumped down the steps toward the larger of the three buildings that, with the house, comprised the only ranch structures.

"Don't forget to bring that saddle in tonight so you can soap it down," Casey called after him as she swung the screen door open to enter the house.

The empty milk pitcher and the white-filmed glass stood silently on the kitchen table amidst the cookie crumbs. Casey shook her head in hopelessness as she cleared the table and wiped it off. There was no doubt that she'd be glad when her mother came back. Next to cooking and cleaning, she hated washing dishes the most. She and Mark had been lucky with the neighbors pitching in to provide precooked casseroles and desserts after their father's accident on Monday and their mother's departure to Scottsbluff so she could be at his side during the recuperation from the operation to insert a pin in his hip. Tonight, however, Mark had devoured the last of the neighbors' offerings. Casey walked to the sink, then groaned as she realized that she had forgotten to get any meat out of the freezer for the evening meal.

If that had happened to her mother, which it never would, she would have been able to raid the refrigerator of its leftovers and the shelves of their tinned supplies and come up with a delicious meal. Casey took one look inside the refrigerator at the spoonfuls of leftovers and knew she could never do it. Bacon and eggs and hash browns, she decided. A person couldn't go wrong with that, Casey thought, as she removed the dish of cold potatoes from its shelf.

Nearly an hour later, she heard two large thumps coming from the barn which doubled as a stable. That meant Tally, her buckskin horse, had just finished his grain. Ever since he was a yearling, he had kicked the back of his stall twice the minute he had finished his oats, another personality quirk that made horses into individuals. If Mark was on schedule, he would be in to dinner in fifteen min-utes.

Casey turned the fire on under the grated pota-toes, flipped the sizzling bacon over in the second skillet and added a spoonful of lard to the third skillet. The table was already set, the toaster sitting to one side with slices of her mother's homemade bread in the compartments. Opening the refrigera-tor, she placed a half dozen eggs in a bowl while juggling the jar of preserves in her other hand. She was beginning to feel very efficient as she sat the bowl of eggs by the stove and the preserves on the table. She popped the slices of bread into the toast-er, stirred the potatoes around so that they browned evenly and straightened out the curling bacon. Remembering that Mark liked his eggs turned over easy so that the yolks remained runny, Casey lit the fire under the last skillet and removed a small saucer from the cupboard to break the eggs in as she had seen her mother do many times before.

When she tapped the first egg on the saucer's edge, it broke smoothly, then she dropped the shell into the saucer accidentally. The ragged edge of the shell broke the yolk of the egg. Grimacing but thinking that she didn't really mind eating hard cooked eggs, she slid it in the skillet. But when the second, third and fourth eggs met the same fate under different circumstances, Casey lifted her hands in despair, vowing that Mark could eat scrambled eggs and like it. Hurriedly she broke the remaining eggs into the skillet and began stirring them together as fast as she could with a fork. Simultaneously she smelled the bacon burning and heard the toast pop up. As quickly as she could, she transferred the barely charred bacon strips onto a towel to drain, stirred the increasingly crisp hash browns and ran to the table to butter the toast, before suddenly remembering the eggs.

Mark walked into the kitchen, took one look at Casey as she muttered to herself between trips from the stove to the table and shook his head in disbelief.

"Wouldn't it have been much simpler to go to town and eat?" he asked, his eyes glancing sadly into Casey's angry gaze, before returning to the too crisp hash browns, the burnt bacon, the globs of unmelted butter on the cold toast and the scorched eggs. "I don't understand how Mom could have possibly had a daughter who's as rotten a cook as you."

"Just shut up and eat!" She jerked her chair away from the table and sat down, trying not to look too closely at the unappetizing food before them.

"It was bad enough last night." Mark's voice croaked as he rose from his chair to open the refrigerator door and take out a bottle of ketchup. "When you boiled the potatoes dry and forgot to turn the oven on to heat Mrs. Gordon's meat casserole." The hash browns snapped like potato chips when he touched them with his fork. "But an entire meal cooked by you?"

Casey was chewing the rubbery eggs with false contentment, wondering if she swallowed them whether they would go all the way down. She glanced over at her brother just as he picked up a more thoroughly charred piece of bacon and it crumbled in his hand.

"When's mom coming home?" he moaned.

"Not until Sunday," Casey replied in an equally depressed tone.

The two pairs of eyes met and with one motion they rose from the table.

"With both of us helping, we can clean the kitchen up in ten minutes and be at the restaurant within an hour," Mark vowed.

CHAPTER THREE

CASEY WAVED GOODBYE to Mark as he set out on his bay gelding. It was nearly five miles from the house to the graveled road where the school bus picked him up. And Mark believed wholeheartedly in the western motto: "Never walk when you can ride." He was counting the days until his sixteenth birthday when he could get his driver's licence and not be forced to take the bus. That time wasn't a long way off either, Casey sighed, just five months away.

Sam Wolver, their hired hand, was already hammering away at a horseshoe beside their portable blacksmith equipment. Unwillingly Casey glanced at the horse tied to the nearby post. It was Injun Joe, the horse that had thrown her father. Studying him from the rear, she admired again the almost perfect quarter horse conformation. His coffee-brown coat gleamed in the morning sun while his nearly black tail swished idly at the flies. He should have been a bay horse with black points, but his legs were snow white from his hooves to about four inches above his knees. The horse swung his head around as he heard Casey's boots making their soft sound on the mixture of sand and gravel. She couldn't suppress the shudder that went through her as she stared at the almost totally white face with just a small amount of coffee-brown color visible on his cheeks. A changeling, her father had called him and Casey agreed, especially when she looked into his eyes. One was brown and one was blue.

Just meeting the horse's gaze was unnerving. She had often argued with her father to sell him, but he had always pointed out what a good cowhorse he was. It was true. Injun Joe was probably the best cutting horse on the ranch. Any time he was near a herd of cattle, it was a joy just to sit back in the saddle and let him work. It was the rest of the time that Casey was uncomfortable with him. He was totally unpredictable at any other time and couldn't be counted on to perform the simplest task.

The day of the accident, Casey had tried to persuade her father to take her buckskin out to check the well in the near pasture since his favorite mount was lame. But he had insisted on taking Injun Joe, who hadn't been ridden since the spring roundup nearly a month before.

She hadn't liked the way the horse had set off with such a stiff-legged walk. Casey knew she never wanted to relive the moment nearly three hours later when she saw the empty saddle on the horse when he wandered into the yard. The terror that had gripped her with its ice-cold fingers had practically numbed her voice. Her knees had shaken so badly when she mounted her own horse that she had trouble holding him. Thankfully Smitty had been there. It was his calmness that had finally settled her down enough so that she was able to backtrack her father's trail while Smitty followed in the pickup.

Together they had found her father trying to crawl back to the main track in the pasture. His face white with pain, he had told them what had happened. How the horse had done some minor bucking when they first reached the pasture meadow. How John Gilmore had been lulled into thinking that the friskiness, or whatever it was, was over, then without warning the horse had suddenly lowered his head and began bucking in earnest. In the first jump, her father had lost a stirrup and by the second, he had already started his flight through the air. Only his retelling of the escapade wasn't so mildly worded.

Casey shook off the unpleasant memory with an effort. She hurried quickly toward the corral where her buckskin waited, already saddled and ready to go. The rich golden-yellow color of his coat was beautifully complemented by his black mane and tail and black-stockinged feet. Docilely he followed her as she took his reins and led him out of the corral to the waiting horse trailer. The dog Shep was sitting beside the pickup, somehow man-

aging to have all four feet beating an anxious tat-
too while still not moving from his place. Once she
had the horse securely tied in the trailer Casey
gave the command for Shep to get into the back of
the pickup. He needed no further word, obeying
the command with alacrity.

Once Casey hopped into the cab of the truck,
she tooted the horn twice at Sam to let him know
she was leaving. He had been working so long for
them, nearly ten years, that he no longer needed to
be told what to do or when to do it. As long as it
wasn't mechanical, Sam Wolver could do anything
on the ranch and ably, too.

Silent Sam, Mark called him. They didn't really
know very much about him. He didn't seem to
have any family that he cared about. He had
refused offers to sleep in the bunkhouse, choosing
instead to park a ramshackle trailer alongside one
of the ranch's so-called lakes, which were really
more like large ponds. Sam never talked much,
hence his nickname, but when he did, you could
bet it was important or informative. He had an
"Old West" attitude toward women, treating them
with the utmost respect and courtesy. Casey had
more than once thought his behavior toward her
mother was almost worshipful. She had the feeling
that he was the last of a mold of men that had
shaped the western frontier. Long and lean and
shy and well-versed in the vagaries of Mother
Nature's plants and animals, he had told Casey of

the different plants that grew in the Sand Hills, of the uses that they had been put to by the Indians who once roamed the area, and of the time when the bison had ruled these prairies, their numbers mounting into the millions.

Casey remembered how Smitty and Johnny used to tease her when she was younger that Sam was an orphan from a wagon train that had been raided by the Indians, that Sam had been captured and raised as an Indian himself. His nearly ageless façade and his amazing lore had convinced her for a time until her father had at last explained that it was impossible. Still, that was the way Sam Wolver appeared to her and always would—a throwback to a bygone era and another breed of men.

Casey was almost to the gate at Burnt Hollow pasture when she saw the dust of Smitty's pickup approaching from the opposite direction. By the time he had parked his pickup and trailer behind hers, she already had Tally unloaded and was opening the gate. Smitty, like Casey, wasted no time in unloading his horse and leading him through the gate. They both knew work came first and talk afterward. Once the gate was firmly closed, they mounted, both horses setting out in a ground-eating trot with Shep's feathery tail waving merrily in front of them.

They followed the fence for some distance before Smitty broke the companionable silence.

"What did Mark say when you told him about the new man coming?"

"You know Mark. The most major catastrophe
in his life was when he thought he was never going
to grow any taller." Casey laughed easily, before a
slight frown that had nothing to do with the bright
morning sun creased her forehead. "He seemed
relieved that he wouldn't have so much work to do
this summer. I guess it's a natural reaction for
someone as young as he is."

"So the wise old woman says," Smitty teased,
"with the learned wisdom of her years."

Casey blushed lightly, recognizing the patroniz-
ing note that had been in her voice. The slight bud-
ding of color in her cheeks gave her a very
feminine glow that seemed at odds with the boyish
jeans and boots and the plain blouse. Her hair was
bared to the sun which illuminated the brown
color with a golden sheen. The gentle breeze
fluffed the close-cropped curls so that dainty swirls
kissed her face. Dark, naturally arched brows had
never known a tweezer to ensure their graceful
shape. Her brown eyes that sometimes seemed to
snap with angry fires were warm and almost shy.
The sprinkling of freckles across her nose and
cheeks seemed to have been dusted on her tanned
skin to give her the air of pert innocence. Although
her mouth was small in keeping with the rest of her
features, her finely shaped lips were pleasingly generous.

"There's the break in the fence!" Casey pointed.

Directly ahead of them stood a tree beside the

fence. Hard cold winters and hot dry summers had shorn it of its foliage and stripped it of its bark. The whiteness of its sun-bleached trunk stood out sharply against the green gold color of the rolling prairie. One large limb had been torn from the tree and now lay at its base, taking with it a section of fence as it fell.

Quickly Casey and Smitty secured their ropes around the branch, wrapping the free end around their saddle horns and towing it away from the fence. Once it was out of the way, they cleared away the tangle of snapped barbed wire. As they remounted and rode their horses through the gap, Smitty indicated the direction where he believed he had seen the Anchor Bar cattle.

The deceptively flat hills stretched out before them. Any depression could successfully hide a full-grown cow from view, or a horse and rider. Here and there, wind had eroded away the sturdy prairie grass from the side of a small hill, exposing the tan-colored ground that gave the Sand Hills their name. A meadowlark trilled out its "Hey, Jiminy Whittaker!" call while a sharp-tailed grouse burst into the air a few feet ahead of them.

A godforsaken land, Casey had heard it called by some people who stared at the vast expanse of sky and the unbroken rolling hills and cried out at the isolation it implied. But Casey heard the whisper of wind, the melodic calls of the birds and the quiet shuffle of her horse's hooves as it moved over the grass and sand. She loved to rise early in the morning and watch the sun penetrating the mists and the kaleidoscope of colors as the sun settled on the western horizon at the end of the day. This was her home; there was no loneliness. How could there be when she was surrounded by the people she loved and the sights and sounds that were set on this earth by God?

As the two riders topped the crest of a hill, they both saw the small group of cows grazing on the rich grass in the hollow. The white faces lifted warily as Casey and Smitty slowly approached the herd. Shep trailed silently behind them, his mouth opened in a happy grin as he panted from the warmth. His bright eyes studied the cows thoroughly as he waited very patiently for his mistress to signal to him to round them up.

"I count seven Anchor Bar brands," Casey spoke softly.

Smitty nodded agreement as they circled the herd and saw three more that had wandered off from the main group. Casey's hand swept out before them and Shep darted forward, snapping and biting at the cows as he began his work of bunching them together. The dog was a whirlwind, dashing and springing from one to another until they were all together in a loosely grouped circle. Now Casey and Smitty nudged their horses forward, separating the Anchor brands from the Bar S. Shep lay silently in the grass, moving only when an Anchor Bar cow threatened to join a retreating member of the Bar S.

"I swear that dog can read brands," Smitty declared, when the last cow had been cut away and they began to drive the ten head back toward the gap in the fence.

"He gives you an awfully eerie feeling sometimes," Casey agreed, smiling at the dashing black and tan dog racing alongside the cattle.

The pace back to the fence was brisker than the first. In half the time they were back and had driven the cattle on to the Gilmore ranch. Another hour was spent patching the broken strands of barbed wire so that the fence was once more secure.

"I've got a thermos of lemonade in the pickup," Casey invited as Smitty shoved a pair of pliers back in his saddlebag.

"And I can use it!" he exclaimed, wiping the perspiration from his forehead with the back of his hand.

"I'll race you back."

Casey didn't bother to accept his challenge verbally. She just grabbed the buckskin's reins and vaulted into the saddle with Smitty only a split second behind her on his mount. Her horse nearly jumped out from under her as she drove her heels into his flanks. Smitty's bay was as fast as her own fleet Tally. Most of the way back to the trailers they raced stride for stride, dodging the clumps of yucca bushes or jumping them when they had to save time. But Casey's lighter weight eventually forecast the winner and she began to draw away as they neared the pasture gate. When they reined in their horses, she had won by more than a length.

"Loser cools the horses!" she announced with a gleeful hoot.

"As long as the winner pours out the lemonade, I don't mind." Smitty took her reins with a grin.

Casey rejoined him a few minutes later, exchanging a cup of cold lemonade for the reins of her horse, then fell in step with him as they made the slow circle to cool their heated horses.

"I was telling dad last night about your father's arrangement for a ranch man while he's in the hospital. When dad plagued me for more specific details which I couldn't supply, he called the hospital long distance last night. Do you know who's coming out here?" Smitty asked, looking down at the grim-faced girl walking beside him.

"No, I don't. And I don't care," she retorted, keeping her face expressionless.

"Flint McCallister." Smitty paused, letting the name sink in. Casey continued walking, staring blankly ahead of them without commenting on his statement. "You know who he is, don't you?"

"I can't say that I do." Her reply was cool, letting him know of her dislike of the subject.

"The McCallister Land and Cattle Company of Ogallala! Every cattleman in the midwest has heard of them."

"Oh, them." Casey's nose turned up disdainfully.

"Don't try to tell me you're not impressed by the news," Smitty persisted. "You've heard talk yourself of how old man McCallister and his son could have taken the whole Sand Hills area and acquired the biggest cattle empire in the United States during the drought years. Instead he went out of his way to help every rancher he could, even to extending them credit when he couldn't afford it himself. He very nearly went under along with some of the others. Flint McCallister is his grandson." He noticed the grudging expression of admiration on Casey's face. "Don't you remember a couple of years ago when Flint McCallister took part in that exchange program and spent a year in Australia studying their methods of ranching in the Outback on—what do they call their spreads—stations?"

"I remember," Casey muttered. "It's really going to be quite a comedown for him to be in charge of our measly sixteen thousand acres."

"Good grief, Casey! Can't you stop being so bitter and realize the opportunity that you're going to have!" Smitty exclaimed. "Think of how much you can learn from this man while he's here! Why, it's rumored that his father is stepping down this winter and giving Flint complete control of the company."

"And how can you be so blind!" Casey hurled

her angry words at him. "Can't you just see how the 'great man' is going to lord it over us with his high and mighty airs? You're looking at one girl who isn't going to be bossed around by that know-it-all!"

Smitty compressed his lips grimly. It was absolutely useless arguing with her. She could be so bull-headed and obstinate that it would only lead to more harsh words. Instead he determinedly led his horse over to the trailer and loaded him up, knowing that the slightly muffled sounds indicated that Casey was doing the same.

"I'll follow you to the ranch and pick up that motor that broke down," he said curtly before climbing into the cab of his truck.

Casey nodded an angry agreement, shooting the bolt that held the trailer's loading chute in place.

CHAPTER FOUR

FLINT MCCALLISTER—Flint McCallister—Flint McCallister! Casey felt if she heard that name one more time, she'd explode. The entire weekend that name had been on the lips of everyone who had visited her father at the hospital. Her father had become more and more pleased with the thought that this man was going to run his ranch. He seemed to take pride that someone as well known and respected as Flint McCallister was the new boss man for the Anchor Bar. The enthusiasm of his fellow friends and ranchers added to his satisfaction. The awe and reverence in their voices when they spoke his name had disgusted Casey. They were referring to him as if he were the President of the United States, a famous film star and God all rolled into one.

Johnny had come down Sunday. He had been particularly elated by the news since it removed the feelings of guilt that had been plaguing him. Casey had been right when she had decided there was no use appealing to her brother to prevent the new man from coming. Johnny was one hundred percent in favor of it. Even Mark had caught the contagious rush to praise this paragon called Flint McCallister. He had beleaguered Casey on the drive home Sunday with their mother with all the tales he had heard about him. Her mother was the only one who noticed her grim silence as Casey fought to control her rising temper. But there was no comfort in meeting the sympathetic glance. She knew too well that Lucille Gilmore was happy that a man was coming to run the Anchor Bar.

This morning Casey had been in her father's office using the phone to check with Smitty about the broken pump for the number ten well. It was called an office since it housed the ranch's records and a desk. It had been intended as a dining room, situated just off the kitchen, but it had never been used as such. It had just naturally become the ranch office where John Gilmore had installed his gun cabinet, decorated the walls with his hunting trophies and his favorite easy chair. In recent years an old day bed was added as the bookwork increased and more and more late hours were kept by her father in that room.

Just as Casey had hung up the telephone receiver, her mother entered the room, her arms loaded with dust rags, mops and polish. Casey hadn't really paid a great deal of attention to her until she was halted in the doorway by her mother's words.

"There are some fresh sheets and blankets on the hallway table, Casey. Would you bring them in?"

"What for?" She watched her mother remove the coverlet from the daybed.

"So I can change the bedding," her mother replied. There was a slight pause as Mrs. Gilmore looked dubiously at the exposed mattress. "On second thoughts, why don't you take the mattress outside and air it for me instead?" Her hand reached out in an absentminded gesture. "And you'd better lend me a hand to bring that cupboard of your grandmother's in from the bunkhouse. We'll need Sam to help with that. But you and I can manage that small dresser in the attic." Her mother's eyes drifted around the room in studied concentration as Casey slowly realized what was happening. "I think we can arrange the furniture so that it will fit in satisfactorily and still give him plenty of room for his clothes."

"You mean *he* is going to say here in *this* room!" Casey exploded. "What's wrong with the bunkhouse where all the rest of the hired help stay? Why does he have to live in the house with us?"

"Mr. McCallister is not exactly hired help, Cassandra." There was a sharp reprimand in Lucille Gilmore's quiet voice. She only used Casey's given name when she was particularly upset with her daughter.

"But this is dad's room!" Angry tears pricked her eyes as Casey realized that this Flint McCallister was not only usurping her father's position but his personal office as well. Venomous, biting and hateful words rose in her throat, only to be stopped by the pitying and reproving look in her mother's eyes.

"I thought you'd got over this feeling of antagonism. We're very lucky to be getting a man so knowledgeable," she said firmly to her angry daughter.

"I hate him!" Casey's words were drawn through her clenched teeth in a whisper trembling with the violence of her emotion.

"Cassandra Gilmore!" The shocked horror in her mother's tone spun Casey around and sent her speeding out the door. She was not going to hear another lecture on the paragon Flint McCallister.

She shouted to Sam at the barn that he was wanted at the house before she hopped into the cab of the blue and white pickup and slammed the door shut. As the wheels churned up the sand in response to the sudden demand for acceleration, Casey had a brief picture of Sam walking to the house porch, respectfully removing his hat as Mrs. Gilmore walked out, her hand shading her eyes while she watched Casey speed down the lane. She didn't remember turning on to the graveled road and was only half conscious of the squealing of her tires as she turned south on the highway. Not until she reached the turn-off for the Agate Fossil Beds did her rage burn away to leave bitter ashes of suppressed anger. She braked the pickup to a stop near the bridge over the Niobrara River, made a U-turn and headed back for the ranch.

Flint McCallister indeed! She could just picture him dressed in one of those beautifully tailored western suits with a fancy white Stetson hat and soft leather boots of kangaroo hide. He'd be wearing one of those fancy string ties with a diamond-studded clasp in a longhorn design. She'd heard about these big cattle barons before, of their loud bragging talk about the money they'd made and how much they'd lost in weekend excursions to Las Vegas. More than likely this McCallister's father had been glad to send him off to Australia for a year so he wouldn't go through the family fortune. She had known a few of those spoiled grandsons of early pioneers. This man had probably learned long ago how to throw his family name around. It was no wonder that people abroad get the impression that Americans are a loud and bragging group, Casey thought bitterly, because of rotten apples like Flint McCallister in the barrel that's shipped overseas.

In her side vision, she spotted a small herd of pronghorn antelope grazing in a pasture near the road. She tooted her horn, watching their delicate heads raise before they took off with bounding leaps. Her speedometer read nearly sixty and, as they raced alongside the fence, they still kept abreast of her until they finally veered away. The white, targetlike circles of their rumps were in view for only a few seconds before they disappeared behind a hill.

Casey was just cresting a hill when she turned her attention back to the highway. Suddenly there in front of her was a horse trailer and a pickup going at a much slower speed. She had two choices, to slam on the brakes and hope she didn't run into it from the rear, or to pass it. In the split second that it took her to glance ahead to see the highway stretching clear of any traffic save the vehicle ahead of her, Casey turned the wheel out and stepped on the accelerator to ensure her passing the pickup and trailer cleanly before the next hill came up. She had no doubt in her ability as a driver, having started her lessons when she was nine, driving the ranch's tractor and graduating to the pickup as soon as her legs were long enough to reach the floorboards.

There was a small smile of satisfaction on her face as she passed the pickup with plenty of room to spare before the hill loomed before her. The deafening roar of wind from her open windows filled the cab, giving her an exhilarating feeling of victory so that she didn't slacken her speed. On the downhill slope the needle crept to eighty. Without warning, Casey heard a sickening thud at the same time that the steering wheel was nearly wrenched out of her hands. A blowout! With all her strength, she held the wheel on a straight course, removing her foot from the accelerator and slowly applying the brake.

The pickup finally rolled to a halt on the shoulder of the road. Her arms and legs were trembling so badly that she couldn't move. She just rested her head against the steering wheel, mentally chiding herself for speeding, and at the same time trying to cheer herself up that for once the spare tire was in good condition. In the next instant her door burst open and she was staring into the angriest pair of stormy gray eyes she had ever seen. For one ridiculous moment she was reminded of the dark, rolling thunderclouds that sometimes covered the Sand Hills' skies.

"You crazy, idiotic— What was the idea, going that fast? What were you trying to do, kill yourself!! You damned females driving like that are a menace to every sane driver on the road!"

"Well, thanks a lot," Casey jeered, her own short temper rearing up to strike back at this callous stranger. "But no, I'm not hurt. It was kind of you to ask."

"It's usually the other guy that is," the man replied, undaunted by her sarcastic rejoinder. "Where's your tire jack?"

"I'm perfectly capable of changing my own tire," Casey answered, pushing her way out of the cab to reach back behind the seat for the jack. With the disassembled tool in her hand, she gave him a haughty look in return for his of arrogant amusement and mocking disbelief before stalking around the pickup to the right front wheel.

She didn't attempt to hide her glowering expression as she heard his footsteps following her. She had the jack assembled in seconds and quickly raised the front end of the pickup truck. She began to unscrew the nuts holding the wheel of the flat tire in place. The first one popped loose immediately, but the second one refused to budge. Casey could feel the stranger's eyes watching her. Unwilling color crept into her cheeks as she hit it to try to knock it free. Her palm stung sharply with the blow, but the nut refused, despite all her hard efforts, to budge.

Before she could stop him, he had pushed her out of the way.

"I can do it!" she protested angrily.

"So I see," he said as he deftly hit the handle of the wrench and unscrewed the nut. "If you want to be useful, you can get the spare tire."

Casey's fists doubled up in anger as she went to retrieve the spare. His authoritative tone ruffled her hair the wrong way. By the time she returned, he had the flat tire removed and expertly rolled the spare in place. For the first time Casey had the opportunity to study the man who had so unwelcomely forced his assistance on her.

The straw cowboy hat was set well back on his head, revealing thick brown hair interlaced with burnished red highlights. The profile was strong and masculine from the smooth forehead and straight nose to the square-cut jaw and finely honed chin. His eyebrows were dark like his hair and the left seemed to be perpetually arched in mockery. And his eyes were so dark a gray that in the shadows they nearly appeared black. His skin was deeply tanned from many hours in the sun, making a sharp contrast to the white shirt he wore. Casey remembered that he had been quite tall in that brief moment that she had stood beside him, six feet or perhaps an inch or two more. Long and lean, she thought, studying the muscular spread of his back and the slim-hipped and well-worn Levis.

"There you are." He rose to his feet, went over, released the jack and disassembled it before handing it back to her. There was the barest hint of a smile on his face and two creases that could have been called dimples on any other person, but on him, Casey felt, they emphasized the sarcastic mockery in his eyes.

She watched him effortlessly place the flat tire in the back of the pickup while she quietly stowed the jack away.

"And *you're* very welcome, too," he drawled when Casey failed to thank him for his help.

"I never asked you to help me," she retorted.

"My mistake." He touched his hat in mock respect. "I won't make it again. Drive a little slower. Next time you might not be so lucky."

Casey jumped quickly into the truck, turning the ignition on hurriedly. She grinned into the side mirror as she trod on the accelerator and drove away. Nobody told her how to drive!

CHAPTER FIVE

AFTER SHE HAD put some distance between herself and the pickup and horse trailer, Casey slowed down to a more moderate speed. Not for anything would she have admitted to that infuriating cowboy that the blowout had frightened her a little. Why did it seem as if the whole world was against her just because she was a female? Even he had made a derogatory remark about idiot females. It was no wonder that there was a woman's liberation movement!

The truck's pace when it was finally turned up the lane that led to the house was considerably slower than when it had left. Casey drove it over to the ranch's fuel drums to fill the nearly depleted gas tank. She noticed Sam at the corral, his gentle hands calming one of the yearlings he had begun to halter break. Evidently her mother had completed all the various shiftings of furniture to prepare for the arrival of Mr. Flint McCallister. Once the tank was filled, Casey drove the truck over to the one big shade tree in the yard and parked it. Shep appeared from his wanderings to welcome her home with suitable enthusiasm.

Casey had just put one foot on the porch step to enter the house when she heard the sound of another vehicle coming up their lane. For the first few minutes a dust cloud obscured it from her vision as it rounded the curve of the hill. Shep's acute hearing failed to recognize the motor's sound as any that had been to the ranch before. The long hair on his back raised up as he bravely raced forward to challenge the intruder.

Her hands moved to rest on her hips in a disgusted and angered stance as Casey recognized the pickup truck and trailing horse van. The curve of her mouth turned down in a grim line. The pickup braked to a stop in front of the house and the tall stranger who had helped her change the tire hopped out, undaunted by the ferocious warning from Shep.

"It wasn't necessary for you to follow me," Casey spat out sarcastically. "I was quite capable of making it back without your assistance."

"This is the Gilmore ranch, isn't it?" There was a husky quality to the low, baritone voice that carried a commanding tone.

"Yes, it is. But if you're looking for work, you can just climb right back in your truck and move on, because we aren't hiring," Casey replied sharply. "And if we were, we wouldn't want any drugstore cowboys."

Their two pairs of eyes clashed in silent challenge while Shep growled menacingly at the stranger. Even though the anger was definite in the man's gray eyes, Casey was surprised to see a glint of amusement as if she were a kitten trying to prevent a mountain lion from crossing her path. This stranger was nothing more than a common trespasser, Casey thought with undisguised contempt.

"Did I hear a car drive in?" her mother's voice asked a second or two before the screen door to the house swung open. Before Casey had a chance to reply, Lucille Gilmore saw the stranger standing in front of the snarling dog. Her hands clapped together sharply as she called the dog away and cast her daughter a scolding glance. The stranger politely removed his cowboy hat, revealing again the thick brown hair which occasionally mirrored the sun's fire.

"Mrs. Gilmore?" He stepped forward.

"Yes, yes, I am. What can we do for you?" Her mother's melodic voice instantly revealed the open-armed friendliness that was so natural to her.

"My name is McCallister, Flint McCallister."

The announcement took both of them by surprise. But it was Casey's reaction that he was watching. Her hands slid off her hips while her squared shoulders sagged in disbelief. If her mouth had dropped open, her astonishment couldn't have been more obvious.

"We didn't expect you until the middle of the week," her mother was saying, while Casey continued staring at the stranger who bore no resemblance at all to the Flint McCallister she had imagined.

"I hope I haven't inconvenienced you."

"Not at all. I just took some homemade bread out of the oven and the coffee pot is always on. Won't you come in?" Lucille Gilmore smiled.

"I'd like to take care of my horse first." He motioned toward the trailer. "Then I'd be happy to."

"My daughter, Cassandra, will show you where you can stable him," her mother offered, much to Casey's disgust. For one thing her mother had used that hated given name of hers and second because Casey wasn't the least bit interested in showing this man anything around the ranch. However she was in no position to disagree.

Her rebellious eyes met his amused glance for a brief instant before Casey moved away from the steps toward him. The sound of the screen door closing told her that her mother had gone back into the house. Her gaze remained fixed on the ground as she walked to the rear of the trailer where the stranger Flint McCallister had already disappeared. All the antagonism she had felt for the man McCallister before she had met him and for the stranger who had so arrogantly thrust his help on her had suddenly been rolled together into one giant ball of hatred. Her eyes were two bright pieces of coal, throwing off dark sparks as he led his horse out of the trailer.

Any other time Casey would have fallen in love with the horse. It was a blue black Appaloosa, with only its rump carrying a blanket of white to exhibit the circular spots of black. Now all she could think about was that anyone could have an animal like that *if* they had the money to buy one. If she had thought about it before, Casey was sure she would have picked a horse like this for McAllister to own, a flashy and showy mount to draw attention to himself.

"I imagine you'll want a stall to keep him in," were the only words she could say aloud. "Our ranch horses just run loose in the corral with a shed for shelter."

"He's a stallion. I prefer to have him penned separately," Flint McCallister replied, his tone just as short and to the point as Casey's. "A stall won't be necessary."

"Sam, our hired man, can fix up something for you." She motioned towards the barn. "He's working with some of the yearlings this morning."

The Appaloosa followed docilely at the end of the lead rope as they walked toward the building. Sam was leaning against one of the corral posts, a homemade cigarette dangling out of the corner of his mouth as he talked softly to the yearling colt standing beside him. Casey never liked to interrupt these intimate sessions when the colt's ears were perked, listening intently to every word that came from Sam. There was no need to let him know they

were standing on the other side of the corral
because Sam would already know. She glanced at
Flint out of the corner of her eye, half expecting
him to show impatience. He wasn't. He was watching with the same rapt attention that she usually
did as the wizened cowboy performed his magic on
the young horse. Finally Sam straightened and led
the horse to the pasture gate, removed the lead
rope and swatted the horse on the rump as it
sprang through toward the open field.

When Sam turned back toward them, Casey
watched his face eagerly, anxious to see his reaction to the new boss man. Whatever Sam thought
as he shook the hand extended to him after Casey's
introductions was securely hidden behind his ageless face. The meeting of the two men was over in a
matter of minutes with Sam walking away leading
the Appaloosa. The toe of her boot dug into the
sand as Casey turned reluctantly toward the house.
She had hoped to rid herself of McCallister's company by pawning him off on Sam. She had been
sure that he wouldn't allow Sam to care for his val-
uable horse without him watching. But Flint
turned with her.

"I saw your father this morning. We went over
quite a few things, but I'm going to be grateful for
your help over these next few weeks, Cassandra."

Casey gave him a malevolent glance. What was
she supposed to do, grovel at his feet for throwing
her a little bit of candy when the whole piece
should have been hers?

"It's kind of you to say so." Her lips curled in bitter sarcasm. "Especially to a female." She ignored the raised eyebrow. "Would you tell mother that I'm going into Harrison to get the tire fixed. I'll have lunch there."

Casey wheeled abruptly away. Let the others make him welcome, she thought bitterly. She wasn't going to; there were going to be no false words from her. He was an interloper, unwanted and distrusted.

As she turned the truck toward the lane, she saw him staring after her. She could see by his stance the rigid anger at her rudeness. Yet his head was tilted slightly to the side in what seemed like curious amusement.

RETURNING FROM TOWN, Casey met Smitty en route to her ranch. He honked his horn and motioned toward the rear bed of his truck. She had a fleeting glimpse of a motor sitting in the back. He had evidently fixed the pump motor for the number ten well. She waved for him to follow her and set her course for the track leading off their lane to the number ten well.

"What are you looking so glum about today?" Smitty asked as he unloaded the motor to restore it to its former position.

"*He's* here," Casey said meaningfully, a serious frown marring her features.

"McCallister? Flint McCallister?" He exhaled

slowly in a silent whistle as he paused in his efforts. "Now that you've met the big boss man, what do you think of him?"

"He's not big," she snorted. "He's just tall, that's all." In despair, she turned away and leaned against the pickup's fender. "Oh, Smitty, he's even worse than I imagined!"

Gently Smitty coaxed her into explaining her statement. All the while she told him about the meeting on the highway, he maintained an outward calm, his hands busy fastening the motor in place. He could hear the trembling dismay in her voice at the impotence of her anger toward Flint McCallister. Smitty knew how Casey hated anyone to watch her when she succumbed to the more feminine side of her nature, treating it as a form of cowardice.

"It was just horrible!" she ended in a defiant flare of temper. "He treated me as if I was a feather-brained female without an ounce of sense. You can just imagine what he thinks of a woman running a ranch! I could tell what an autocrat he was when he so patronizingly asked for my help!"

"Now how do you know that's how he felt?" Smitty accused, coming to stand beside her. "Why can't you accept the fact that the man wants your help? You're the one who has a paranoid inferiority complex."

"I do not!"

"Then why do you take every comment as a personal slur at your sex?" Smitty smiled to take the sting out of his words.

"That is not true! How did this situation come about in the first place? Because I wasn't a man!" Casey trembled in anger. "That's why dad had to hire someone else to come out here—to please those male chauvinist pigs who don't think a woman is capable of running a ranch! And that... that man agrees with them. I can tell."

"You're as open-minded as a bigot." Smitty shook his head in despair. "Take me back and introduce me to this tyrant who's taken over your ranch."

"With pleasure."

But Casey didn't have an opportunity to do so. When they returned to the ranch, Mrs. Gilmore informed Casey, a little sharply, that Mr. McCallister had gone on a self-conducted tour of the property.

"It was really your place to show him around, Casey," her mother reprimanded.

Despite the rebellious glint in her eyes, Casey did lower her gaze guiltily. Lucille Gilmore's gentle reproof made pinpricks of discomfort at her childish behavior. Although Casey was loath to admit she had been in error, she did manage a mumbled apology.

"You don't need to apologize to me," Mrs. Gilmore said, "but to Mr. McCallister."

"When will he be back?" Casey asked grimly.

"I told him supper would be at six."

"Well, I can't stay that long," Smitty stated. "I may stop back this evening to meet Casey's new boss man." A lopsided grin was turned teasingly on Casey, who wrinkled her nose in answer. "Walk me to the truck?"

"WHAT'S HE LOOK LIKE?" Mark persisted, hanging over the side of the manger where Casey was milking their cow, Maisy.

"Oh, I don't know. He's tall, probably six foot one or two, taller than Johnny." She tried to stem her growing exasperation over her brother's questions. "Good looking in a sarcastic and conceited sort of way. What does it matter what he looks like?"

Mark shrugged off her question. "How old is he?"

"How should I know? I didn't ask for his vital statistics."

"Ah, come on. Take a guess?"

"In his early thirties, then." Casey slapped the cow on its side as she moved the bucket away and rose from her stool.

"He sounds interesting." Mark smiled at the answering grimace on his sister's face when she handed him the milk pail.

"Good grief, Mark, you act as if he's Paul Newman! He's just the conceited, arrogant son of a wealthy rancher who's playing at being a cowboy!" Casey retorted. The sound of a vehicle in the

yard was accompanied by Shep's frantic barking.
"That's probably the great man now."

Mark started for the door, slowing his pace
when Casey reminded him not to spill the milk.
She tarried in the barn as long as she could, fussing
with the horses that Mark had already grained
before finally heading toward the house. It was
nearly six o'clock. And when her mother said supper would be ready at six, it was. Her delaying tactics had evidently worked, for when she finally
stepped into the kitchen there was no sign of Flint
McCallister. Casey quickly set to work, washing
her hands before helping her mother place the hot
dishes on the table. Seconds later Mark walked
into the room, directly followed by Flint McCallister.

Casey took pains to keep her glance from sliding
toward him. Inside she felt her anger, frustration
and self-pity warring against each other. Yet all
her senses were keenly tuned to his presence. The
scent of soap and shaving lotion mingled with the
odour of roast beef, while out of the corner of her
eye she could see the crisp white shirt contrasting
with the darkness of his hair still glistening wetly
from a shower. She heard the scrape of the chair as
he seated himself at the table and the clear, rich
tone of his voice as he patiently, but interestedly,
answered Mark's questions.

When all the dishes were on the table, Casey had
no option but to seat herself. The only vacant chair

was on his right. She managed a polite smile to go vaguely in his direction, knowing full well that the falseness showed in her eyes. His own gray eyes captured her gaze before he nodded condescendingly in acknowledgement. There was an answering aggressive thrust to her chin as she passed the potatoes to him. Casey was sure her silence didn't go unnoticed by anyone at the table, but her brother Mark's questions were endless, filling the void that she created.

"Tell us about Australia," Mark urged, shoveling a large portion of potatoes onto his plate despite the reproving glance from his mother. "What are the cattle ranches like down there?"

"The two ranches I visited were both in central Australia, the Outback," Flint answered amiably. "The land there is basically flat and arid with little vegetation. The actual work isn't much different from what we do here. Mostly it was a matter of adjusting to the different terms they use. Ranches are called 'stations'. Roundups are called 'musters' and because of the reverse seasons take place in the spring instead of the fall. The biggest difference is that they don't finish their cattle like we do on corn and grains. Consequently when you order a steak, the meat isn't as tender as you're accustomed to here in the States, although it does have a good flavor."

"Did you see a lot of kangaroos?"

Casey glanced at Flint with a look that plainly

dared him to continue monopolizing the conversation with his exploits. His jaw tightened perceptibly at her gaze even as he turned back toward Mark with an indulgent and, Casey was forced to admit, gentle expression.

"Yes, quite a few, but they're considered a nuisance. There's also quite a few wild turkey and wild pigs. The pigs that I saw looked plump enough for a barbecue, but Benedict, the station owner, assured me that they were too diseased to eat." There was no mistaking the rapt look of interest on Mark's face and Flint continued, "The most unwelcome form of wild life is the dingo."

"That's a breed of wild dog, right?" Mark interrupted, eager to show off his own knowledge however meager it was. His attention was all on Flint.

"They breed with domestic dogs, which makes them uncannily intelligent and hard to catch. They travel in packs, roaming wide areas, attacking calves and weaker stock. You could compare them in nuisance value to the coyote, although a dingo is much more vicious and fiercer in combat."

The meal seemed to pass swiftly as Flint McCallister continued to relate happenings during the year he was in Australia. In spite of herself, Casey discovered she was just as interested as her mother and brother. During the short space of time it took to consume their supper she had learned more about Australia by Flint's comparisons to life as she knew it in Nebraska than she had ever learned in world geography class in school. But she maintained an expression of studied disinterest.

"Well, Mrs. Gilmore," Flint said, draining the last of his coffee from the cup, "that was a delicious meal."

"This family operates on first names, Mr. McCallister," Lucille Gilmore inserted, a genuine smile lighting her face. "Call me Lucille."

"Then you'd better forget the Mr. McCallister and call me Flint." Casey watched his smile transform his face from mocking sureness to devastatingly charming good looks. "Since this is my first night here and I'll probably never have another opportunity of a night free from paperwork, I'd like to show my appreciation for the meal by helping with the dishes."

"I take care of that for mother." With this statement, Casey broke her self-imposed silence.

"And she hates every minute of it!" Mark laughed.

The truth of his gibe was all too accurate, but it was a chore that Casey's conscience had insisted she undertake to make up for her lack of help in other household duties.

"In that case she'd probably be glad of some help for a change." For all the lazy regard of his eyes when they rested on her, Casey could feel the piercing challenge in his gaze.

It was on the tip of her tongue to refuse any assistance from him, but the picture of him in front of a sink full of dishes was too beautiful to deny. The thought of him with one of her mother's decorative aprons tied around his waist brought an audacious twinkle out of the depths of her brown eyes as she accepted with mock demureness.

The dishes were started in silence with Flint electing to wash since Casey would know where the dishes belonged once they were dried. Strangely enough, Flint didn't look in the least out of place standing in front of the sink. He seemed to sense Casey's desire to keep a businesslike remoteness between them.

"I noticed the hay field in the west section is about ready for cutting." He finally broke the silence.

"The first of next week, I imagine," Casey agreed stiffly, loathing to agree with him on anything. "It seems earlier this year, but we did cut that field the second week of June last year."

"Your plane is out of commission. I would like to get an aerial view of the ranch so I can get a better idea of the layout." Casey felt his glance rest on her for a minute. "Would it be possible to borrow a plane from the neighbors?"

"I'm sure the Smiths would lend me theirs. I don't know how they'd feel about lending it to a stranger, though." She enjoyed getting her little dig in even if it didn't seem to penetrate his thick skin.

"I didn't intend to fly it myself. Your mother told me you were just as much at home in an airplane as in a saddle." The gray eyes met her startled glance with only the slightest betrayal of amusement. "Naturally I can't see as much of the land as I want if I'm behind the controls."

"I see." She saw all right. She saw that she was going to be at close quarters with that man for two or three hours. And with growing irritation, she also knew that his inspection of the ranch would be very thorough. "When did you want me to arrange this tour?"

"Tomorrow."

Casey's hand paused as she started to withdraw the meat platter from the rinsing water. He certainly wasn't going to give her a chance to get used to the idea.

"I'll check with them to see if their plane will be free. They might have something scheduled."

"They might," Flint agreed, but Casey could almost visualize his tongue pushing at the side of his cheek.

She had been attempting to stall and she was uncomfortably aware that he knew it. The damp towel refused to wipe over the already dry platter again, its balking drawing Casey back to the work at hand. On tiptoe, she stretched her arms toward the third shelf of the cupboard above the sink. Holding the platter in one hand, she tried to push the bowls out of the way with the other. A group of plastic lids cascaded down on her head just as she pulled the glass bowls too close to the edge and they started to fall. Casey leaned heavily against the sink, trying to gain all the extra inches she could, angrily aware that her shirttail was dragging in the rinsing water. As she was trying to figure out how to set the platter down and still rescue the bowls, she glimpsed Flint reacting to her predicament.

His superior height allowed him to reach the third shelf easily. But to do so, he had to stretch his lean frame over the top of Casey's head. The muscular hardness of his body pressing against her brought an incredible rigid tenseness as she tried to control the tingling of her body where it came in contact with him. From outside there was the slamming of a door and Mark's jubilant cry of welcome.

"Hey, Smitty! I figured you'd be over tonight," Mark called in a voice that rang all too clearly in the kitchen. "The new man's giving you some pretty stiff competition. He's already in the kitchen helping Casey with the dishes."

The bowls had been rescued and the platter in place behind them. Casey's face had turned an amazing shade of red as Flint turned his speculating gaze on her and stepped back. She had one fleeting thought of running out on the porch and strangling her loud-mouthed brother before she chose instead to pick up the lids scattered around the floor.

"I take it your boyfriend is here," Flint stated, returning to the sink and the remaining pan.

"It's . . . it's Smitty," Casey tried to say with some degree of composure which had been disturbed by his potent, masculine virility. "Our nearest neighbor."

"The one you're going to borrow the plane from?"

"Yes."

"Good. We can find out tonight if it's available."

CHAPTER SIX

CASEY HAD MADE a concentrated effort to monopolize Smitty and the conversation that evening. She had deliberately steered the subject toward people and places that were known only to them, thus ignoring Flint McCallister. But Smitty had either been obtuse or stubborn, because he had continually switched it back to ranching. Casey had sat back in fuming silence while they discussed seed bulls, irrigation, feed grains and the effects of the weather. And Flint had given her no opportunity to ask permission to use the Smiths' plane. One politely worded question was all it had taken, and Smitty had volunteered almost ecstatically. Afterward, when Smitty and Casey had been left alone by the discreet Mr. McCallister, she had derided Smitty about it.

"The way you acted when you told him he could have the plane any time he wanted it was positively disgusting," Casey had declared. "I could almost see you having a plaque made that says 'Flint McCallister sat here.'"

"Oh, Casey," Smitty had moaned in exasperation, "why do you persist in making mountains out of molehills? Our plane has been at your disposal ever since yours went on the blink. McCallister didn't know that, since you obviously didn't tell him. All I did was assure him of our assistance."

Casey had snorted at Smitty's statement. It had become apparent that she was alone in her stand against Flint McCallister. In one day she had seen the defection of her younger brother. She was quite sure that her mother had fallen under the charm of his rugged good looks. And now Smitty had joined the throng of admirers.

TWO FLEECY WHITE CLOUDS drifted above the Cessna aircraft while Casey stole a glance at the man seated in the passenger seat. She immediately looked into a pair of gray eyes that had been watching her grow more sullen as each of her thoughts had grown more depressing. They had been flying for more than an hour now.

"What else did you want to see?" she asked, refusing to be disgruntled by the fact that he had been staring at her.

"Let's take another run past that pasture in the south section. Make it a little lower this time."

Casey nodded her compliance and expertly put the plane in a side-slip before completing her turn and leveling out eight hundred feet above the ground. Flying was one of her loves. There was exhilaration in feeling the plane respond to her lightest touch, as quickly as a well-trained reining horse. Plus there was a sensation of being detached from the world. In a small plane, there was a serenity that couldn't be duplicated on the ground.

"You're an excellent pilot," Flint told her.

"I know," Casey answered calmly and without conceit.

"Your father told me you're almost indispensable. And he doesn't strike me as the kind of man who would say that if he didn't believe it."

"No, I don't think he would," Casey agreed, feeling a warm glow of pride at the high compliment from her father. "There's the mesa," she pointed out, crabbing into the wind to hold a straight course. "The pasture's just on the other side."

"He seemed to think you could run the ranch quite efficiently by yourself," Flint continued, now gazing out his window at the Sand Hills below.

"I could." There was determination in the lift of her chin as she met his brief glance squarely. "I thought you wanted to inspect the ranch?"

"Partly."

"And partly what?" she persevered.

"And partly I wanted to get to know you better, Cassandra." His voice was nonchalant, but there was a seriousness in his expression that told Casey she was the main object in the trip. "I had the distinct impression that if I'd try to corner you at the ranch you would have managed to escape just as you did yesterday." He glanced briefly around the interior of the plane.

"You must admit that you can hardly walk away from me here."

Casey's lips tightened grimly. "Let's get this straight, Mr. McCallister. I didn't want you here on this ranch. It wasn't my idea, nor my father's. You're here because the bank wanted a *man* in charge." There was a suitable emphasis on the word "man." "To be perfectly honest, I didn't like you very much before I met you, and now that I have—"

"You still don't," he finished for her. "Your actions have made your feelings perfectly clear. But I'm here. And as they say in war, I'm here for the duration."

"How unfortunate for both of us!"

"If that's going to be your attitude, we're going to be in for a rough month and a half." Flint eyed her questioningly. "Or you can accept the fact that I'm merely a temporary stand-in for your father."

You could never fill his shoes, Casey thought bitterly.

"It's really up to you, Cassandra. You can treat me as an outsider or a fellow rancher, much like your neighbors, the Smiths. In either case, I'd like to remind you of that old Indian saying, 'Don't judge a man until you've walked ten miles in his moccasins.'"

Her hands clenched the wheel as she railed inwardly at his arrogant philosophizing. Part of her could recognize the truth of his statement, but the biggest share of her resented the need for any conversation with him.

"As you say, we're both going to have to make the best of a bad situation," she agreed through gritted teeth and a tight smile. "Should I head the plane back to the ranch?"

Flint nodded, his keen gaze missing none of the smoldering anger in her snapping eyes.

"And another thing," Casey added. "From now on you either call me 'Hey, you' or Casey, but don't you ever call me Cassandra again. I hate that name!"

THE DOCTOR HAD ASSURED THEM that John Gilmore was progressing very well. And Casey had to admit that he was in excellent spirits. After Sunday morning church, Flint had volunteered to drive Casey, her mother and Mark down to Scottsbluff, and if Mrs. Gilmore had no objections, he would drive on into Ogallala to visit his parents and pick the Gilmores up that same evening after visiting hours had closed at the hospital. Her mother had quickly fallen in with the plan.

There was a bit more color in her father's cheeks, Casey decided as they walked into the room. His dark eyes sparkled brightly as he grasped his wife's hand and drew her down to lightly brush her lips in greeting. The whispered exchanges of "I missed you" brought an immediate feeling of family warmth to Casey, but it didn't

stop her from glancing at Flint McCallister to see
if he had heard the exchange. He had seen them all
to the room as a matter of courtesy and to look in
on John Gilmore.

The solemnity of his expression assured Casey
that he had overheard. Against her will, she had to
appreciate the fact that he was remaining in the
background until the family had had a chance to
exchange "hellos," even though he must have been
anxious himself to greet John Gilmore and leave to
see his own family.

"You're looking much better, Mr. Gilmore."
Flint firmly shook the hand extended to him.

It grated Casey to hear her father addressed so
respectfully. She would have much preferred that
Flint had adopted a superior attitude, one that
wouldn't have earned the look of approval in her
father's eyes.

"I'm feeling much better," he acknowledged.
"And the name is John, Flint."

"I'm on my way to visit my parents," Flint
smiled after nodding his acceptance of a more
familiar attitude between them. "I wanted to let
you know everything's running smoothly at the
ranch, except for a few long faces over your
absence."

His glance around the family served as a further
explanation of his words, although Casey felt that
his gaze rested a little longer on her than the
others. But she refused to feel guilty.

"I appreciate your stopping by. I know you must be anxious to be on your way—" John Gilmore smiled broadly "—so I won't keep you with endless questions. I'll save them for Casey." Her father winked at her.

But Casey had difficulty meeting Flint's gaze and the dubious look in his gray eyes at her being able to give him an unbiased account.

With a casual statement that he'd be back about eight, Flint left. The promised questions from her father didn't come, because Flint had no more than left and the Smiths arrived.

"I've been trying to make up my mind why Casey wore a dress today." Her father laughed heartily as he shook Smitty's hand. "At first I thought it was for me. Then I decided it was for McCallister. Now you've turned up, Smitty, and I'm thoroughly confused."

Casey colored slightly in anger as she glanced down at the maroon flowered dress she was wearing. It was styled after the dresses worn in the forties with a wide rounded collar and short sleeves that nearly reached her elbow, only the skirt was much shorter than the original version. The style was becoming to her, but not the color, which was too dull.

"I wore the dress to church this morning, dad," Casey stated. "You know how Reverend Carver frowns on pants."

"Oh, that's the reason." But the twinkle in his

eyes teased her outrageously. Casey was furious with herself for failing to respond with the same humor. But, even in jest, it was disgusting for her father to think that she might have worn a dress to impress Flint McCallister. She was the only one who took more than passing notice of the remark and the subject was quite quickly dropped, much to Casey's relief.

Her father was very well known and liked in the district, so Sundays brought him an abundance of visitors. There was a constant shuffling of people in the room to conform to the hospital's limit on the number of persons visiting a patient at a time. The only one who was excluded from the shifting was Lucille Gilmore. And John Gilmore's hand kept her firmly by his side at all times.

Just as the Smiths began to take their leave late in the afternoon, Johnny Gilmore arrived. Smitty immediately took advantage of the situation and cadged a ride home with Casey so that he could spend some time with Johnny. The three, Casey, Johnny and Smitty, ended up going to dinner together for a thorough round of old times and catching up on present news.

"Tell me about this new man," Johnny urged, nearly halfway through their meal. "Dad's roughed me in on his background, but what's he really like?"

"He certainly isn't the ogre that Casey painted him up to be." Smitty cast a disparaging glance across the table to her before turning back to Johnny. "Flint's really a terrific guy. I've been over there several times this week. I swear to God, Johnny, I don't think there's any new technique in ranching today that he can't intelligently discuss the pros and cons about. But he's not pushy or showy with his knowledge, just matter of fact. McCallister never talks down to you, either." Smitty paused, eyeing Casey hesitantly before he continued. "He's not totally business, though. You get the impression that he's been around socially, if you know what I mean."

"Is he good looking?" Johnny asked with a knowing smile and teasing glance at his sister.

"If you like the type," Casey answered in a suitably bored voice.

"Don't you believe her," Smitty laughed. "He's one of those lean, rugged types that look as if they've just stepped out of a movie screen. You can bet he has any number of girls in his little black book just waiting for him to crook his finger."

"You're disgusting!" Casey exclaimed angrily. "The next thing you know you'll be bragging about your conquests. I can believe that Flint McCallister wouldn't have much respect for a woman's reputation, but you two should."

"What did we do to earn that outburst?" Johnny looked at her with considerable amusement.

"Don't mind her." Smitty shook his head. "All

you have to do is mention that guy's name and she loses her temper. The first time she saw him she was speeding down the highway and had a blowout. He read her the riot act. Her hair's been up ever since."

"That has nothing to do with it!" Casey protested, but weakly as she threw her napkin on the table. She fumbled in her purse, finally extracting some bills which she passed to Smitty. "I'm going back up to see dad. Here's the money for my dinner. You two can stay here as long as you like!"

Flint arrived promptly at eight to take them all home. He made no comment about Smitty riding home with them, just nodding a hello as he held the back door of the station wagon open for Smitty, Casey and Mark. Then he helped Mrs. Gilmore into the front seat beside him before sliding behind the wheel himself. Casey's mother immediately engaged him in a conversation about his visit with his parents, their voices not loud enough to include the three in the back seat. That suited Casey just fine.

Somehow she had been seated beside the window directly behind the driver with Smitty in the middle and Mark on the other side. Smitty was strangely silent, Casey thought. Mark pulled his transistor radio out of his pocket, turned it on low volume and leaned back against the door, holding the radio close to his ear. She gazed out the window at the orange sun hovering over the horizon.

She felt discontented and couldn't figure out why. Her eyes roved back to the man in front of her, examining the brown hair curling near the collar of his blue suitcoat. She felt Smitty's arm slide around to settle on her shoulders. It was a warm comfortable feeling to have his arm around her and she turned, a slow pleasant smile lighting her face.

Dear, darling Smitty, Casey thought, taking his hand that rested on her shoulder and bringing it to her lips where she brushed the tips of his fingers. For some reason probably only known to her subconscious mind, her gaze turned to the rear view mirror on the front dash. Dark, angry thunderclouds from Flint's reflection met her gaze. She was stunned by the violence she saw. Almost immediately her mother said something undecipherable to the driver and the expression in his eyes was quickly veiled as he turned to answer her. The insolent disapproval of his look at the innocent caress brought an equally potent reaction from Casey as she rebelliously snuggled closer to Smitty. Several minutes later she peeped through her lashes, her head resting comfortably on Smitty's shoulder. His eyes, as they briefly met hers, were a lighter shade of gray and remarkably indifferent.

The warmth of Smitty's arms and the darkness of the coming night finally lulled Casey into a state of semi-sleep. Not until the steady rhythm of the car slackened its pace did she become aware of her surroundings.

"Did you want me to run you on home now, Smitty?" Flint half-turned in the seat.

"I'll . . . I'll drive him on home from the house." Casey stifled a yawn while straightening in her seat.

"It's after ten now. We were going to get an early start in the morning to cut that hay." His tone sounded casual enough, but there was just enough doubt in it to upset Casey.

"Don't worry. I've been up later than this and still got up at the crack of dawn." The disguised criticism woke Casey completely and she didn't spare her use of sarcasm.

"Suit yourself."

They had made the turn on to the graveled lane to the ranch house. In minutes the station wagon was halted beneath the yard light. The good-nights were said speedily as Casey kissed her mother, spared Mark a cheery wish for a nice night and smiled stiffly at Flint before she slid behind the driver's seat so recently vacated by him.

"See that she drives carefully." Flint raised a one-finger salute to Smitty. His arrogantly dismissive gaze rested briefly on Casey.

Three-quarters of an hour later she was back. Except for the front porch light, the house looked dark. As quietly as she could, Casey crept into the house. There was a sliver of light showing beneath the office door now serving as Flint's bedroom and working quarters. One of the floor boards under the linoleum creaked loudly as she attempted to sneak past. Immediately the room was bathed in light, except where Flint's silhouette blocked it.

"You didn't have to wait up for me." She was angry, but that wasn't the reason her cheeks flooded with a red stain. It was the way his eyes studied her face so thoroughly just as if Smitty's kisses had been marked on her lips with indelible ink.

"I didn't." The muscles in his jaws twitched. "Yes, I did wait up for you. I've seen a sample of your driving. Besides, I had paper work to catch up on."

"Your concern is touching and unwanted. Good night, Mr. McCallister." His unwarranted criticism left a bitter taste in her mouth that rubbed off on her words.

But Flint shook his head in a mixture of anger and exasperation before closing his door.

CHAPTER SEVEN

THE DAY HAD BEEN unseasonably hot even for the first of June. Casey swore that the temperature had reached over the one hundred mark long before midday. She sighed heavily, wondering if it had really been the sun beating down on her head all day or the futility of her own anger that had sapped her self-confidence. She turned the leather band on her wrist to look at her watch. If it was any consolation, it was only four o'clock, and the last of the hay had been cut. She rubbed the back of her neck, stiff with the tension that had been building up these last three days.

In previous years she had enjoyed haying time, hard work and all. As far as Casey was concerned, there wasn't a more pleasing aroma than the smell of fresh-cut hay. But this time—her lips pressed firmly together—this time she hadn't even noticed it. All because of that autocratic Flint McCallister. Every order he had given had grated her nerves until they were raw. It didn't matter what she had been doing, she had felt his eyes watching her, ready to pounce on the slightest showing of female ineptitude. But she had shown him. She had been up and about before anyone else, stayed later in the fields than anyone else, and every aching muscle in her body could attest to it. Now all she wanted to do was get away. Her legs wearily climbed the front porch steps.

"Mom!" She pushed open the screen door into the kitchen.

"Right here, dear." Lucille Gilmore turned from the stove to her daughter. "Are you all done? You certainly look exhausted."

"Would you throw some food in a bag for me? I'm going down to the pond." Casey tried to put lightness in her voice, only to have the frayed edges show.

Her mother studied her thoughtfully. "Yes, of course I will." More gently, "You still haven't reconciled yourself to Flint yet, have you?"

Casey glanced guiltily at her mother. Parents had no right to be able to read their children's minds so well. Instead of replying, she announced that she was going up to her room to change.

When she returned downstairs there was a paper bag sitting on the table and a thermos of lemonade beside it. A tight smile curved Casey's lips at her mother's undemanding thoughtfulness. She hurried out the door to her already saddled horse, carrying the food and drink and a small telescoping fishing rod.

Later, along the sandy shore line of the small pond, Casey set up her camp, her horse tethered in the rich grass near by. The stones from previous fires were still gathered in their protective circle around the darkened ashes. Dry twigs and branches from the cottonwood trees lay alongside. In a few minutes she had a small fire started, her fishing line in the pond waters and was sitting on her saddle blanket, her knees drawn up close to her chest so her chin could rest on them. Her eyes burned with bitter tears of unshed frustration. She couldn't admire the hawk circling in the brilliant blue sky.

She wasn't going to give in to these childish tears, Casey vowed. Even as she sniffed back a sob, she swore anew that Flint McCallister was not going to get under her skin. But it wasn't really a matter of him so much as it was that she was standing alone against him. First her family had deserted her, then Smitty and now Sam. How was she supposed to fight him alone.

With a groan of irritation, Casey heard the sound of a horse approaching. *If Mark has followed me here*, she thought, *I'll brain him! He should be out trailing after his hero.* She rubbed her eyes quickly to wipe away the water that had gathered.

"Catching anything?" It wasn't Mark. It was Flint.

Inside her there was an explosion of anger, erupting with volcanic force as she bounded to her feet.

"Do you have to follow me everwhere!" Casey screamed. "Why can't you just leave me alone!"

"I saw the smoke from your fire. I had no idea you were out here, so the first thing that occurred to me was that there might have been a grass fire started." The tightly controlled voice should have warned Casey, but it didn't. And neither did the muscle twitching along the side of his jaw.

"When you saw it wasn't a grass fire, you could have ridden home again." Her whole body trembled with anger.

She was conscious of him striding toward her, but not until he got close did she see the anger in his face. His eyes resembled the hard, gray stone of his namesake and looked equally capable of throwing off sparks. His hand clamped on to her wrist as he wrenched her around and pushed her forward.

"Do you see that?" Casey's eyes followed his pointing finger, unwillingly obeying the uncompromising voice. She stared blankly at the thistlelike plant at her feet and the snow-white blossom that topped it.

"That?" her derisive voice asked, staring again at the flower that, except for its whiteness, resembled a poppy.

"Go and pick the blossom for me," Flint ordered.

"Are you crazy?" She stared at him unbelievingly. "That's a prickle poppy! There's thorns all over the stem." Casey didn't like the hard line of his jaw or the feeling that the lean muscular body towering above her was held in check by a very tenuous thread, but she didn't back down from her belligerent stand.

"And I've had to put up with your thorns for ten days, my little prickle poppy called Casey! I didn't ask for this job any more than you asked for your father to be injured. But I'm here and I'm going to stay here!" He hadn't released her wrist and his fingers were biting into the bone. But it wasn't the physical pain that was causing the shiver of fear. It was the ominously quiet way Flint was talking.

"And I'm counting the days until you're gone, too!" she retorted, her voice cracking ever so slightly.

"Your father may have taught you a great deal about ranching, but it's quite obvious that he never bothered to teach you any manners!" Her hand was released in a gesture of disgust, as Flint turned away.

"Don't you speak that way about my father!" This time it was Casey's hand that reached out to detain him. The tears that had been burning her eyes now began to cloud her vision. "He's the most perfect father in the world. I'd do anything for him and he'd do anything for me."

"That's where you're wrong, Casey." Flint stared at her with uncomfortable coldness. "You're too selfish to do 'anything' for him."

"That's a lie!" Her vehement denial ended in a choking sob.

"Is it? You can't even bring yourself to be civil to me, let alone friendly. If your father could have had a choice, he would have been just as satisfied having you run the ranch. But we both know he didn't. You don't hear him complaining. You're the sore loser, Casey, and nobody likes a sore loser."

She couldn't meet his gaze. Her eyes stared unseeingly at his scuffed boots. She tried valiantly to argue with herself that what he was saying was untrue. She felt about the size of a sand flea and just about as useful. There was no getting around it—she was a spoiled, selfish, ungrateful brat who didn't deserve or appreciate the things she had. The sound of creaking saddle leather brought her trembling chin up as Casey saw Flint astride his horse, reining him in the direction of the ranch house.

"Flint." Her voice was weak, but he heard it. He stopped his horse and looked back at her. Pride was an enormous lump in her throat, but somehow Casey swallowed it and walked slowly toward him. She didn't wipe the tears from her cheeks, as she tilted her head to look up to him.

"I'm so...sorry...for the way I've acted."

Before she even completed the sentence, she had lowered her head to stare at the ground. She waited for him to throw her apology back in her face, to tell her that it was too late to make amends. Instead a hand was outstretched toward her in friendship.

"Maybe we won't ever be friends, Casey," Flint said, holding the hand she had placed in his gently. "But let's not be enemies."

She nodded, withdrawing her hand from his in embarrassment. A finger lifted her protesting chin until Casey was forced to look into his face. He was smiling that devastating smile that had always been reserved for others. She caught her breath at the potency of his charm.

"That was a hard thing you just did, admitting you were wrong, especially to me. Your father is a stubborn man or he wouldn't be a rancher, but he's fair and honest, too. I didn't believe his daughter could be any different, only a bit more bull-headed, perhaps."

Casey wondered why she had never noticed the twinkle in his eyes or the rugged forthright lines in his face. Two dots of red appeared on her cheeks as she realized she had been staring and liking what she saw. She stepped back hesitantly, not knowing anything more to say and feeling ridiculously shy.

From a near hilltop came a shrill whinny, answered immediately by Flint's horse. Casey wiped the tears off her cheeks, her glance turning toward the first sound. She smiled widely as she saw the white horse tossing his head a hundred yards from them.

"I haven't seen that horse around the ranch," Flint said.

"That's my horse, Mercury." Casey lifted her fingers to her mouth and whistled. A glow of pride lit her eyes as she watched the horse trot toward them, his stride long and swinging, his nose raised to catch the scent of the stranger, and his tail almost unnaturally erect above his rump. His white coat shimmered with health and not until he had stopped in front of Casey was the heavy weight of his years seen. She rubbed his neck fondly while the horse nuzzled the pockets of her blouse. She laughed gaily, extracting the cubes of sugar and offering them to him.

"He's nearly seventeen years old. You can hardly tell it, can you?" Casey glanced at Flint for his affirmation. "He was my first real horse, the first one that didn't have to be whipped to get out of a trot." She hugged the horse's neck affectionately. "He was as fast as the wind. That's why I named him Mercury, after the Roman god with wings on his feet."

Casey glanced hesitantly at Flint, wondering if he thought her childish and silly. But he seemed to be studying her with interest and not amusement.

"I used to be a terrible tomboy," she went on.

"Used to be?" he laughed, but it was a gentle laugh, one that she could join.

"Uhuh. I liked to pretend that Mercury was an Indian pony. I was forever riding him without a saddle or bridle, guiding him with my knees. Most of the time it worked," she grinned.

"He looks in great shape for his age."

"His teeth are beginning to wear down terribly now." A sad note crept into her voice. "Dad said this spring when we wormed him that by the time next summer is over, Mercury probably won't have any teeth left. They'll all be worn to the gum. He likes to run free," she declared fervently, a frown creasing her forehead. "I hate to see the day come when Mercury is reduced to eating mash instead of the rich pasture grass."

The white horse nuzzled her pockets once more in search of any sugar Casey might have overlooked. Deciding there was none, he turned away, trotting out toward the hills from which he had just come.

"It has to happen some time." There was no prophecy in Flint's words, only fact. But Casey sensed the understanding he communicated.

"Yes...yes, I know. He's led a...full life."

Even as she sighed the last words, she smiled. Living on a ranch had taught her that the cycle of life was never-ending; no one could halt it. She had learned to accept the things that weren't in her power to change, although it didn't make them any easier.

It was a new experience for her to be talking so easily to him, one that Casey found unsettling and yet immensely enjoyable. For these few brief moments Flint had made her feel important. Perhaps that was why when he left, she felt just a little bit lonely.

CASEY TOOK THE PORCH STEPS two at a time. The tune, "There's no place like Nebraska," was a merry melody that she hummed to match her buoyant spirits. Finally accepting Flint as a fellow rancher whose interest, like hers, lay in what was best for the ranch had made the difference. Casey found a new enjoyment in working side by side with him which filled her with a previously unknown satisfaction. She also found a certain admiration growing for Flint, one that she still tried to hide, but was becoming increasingly apparent. Just as she opened the kitchen door, Casey heard Mark exclaiming, "No! No!"

He was standing in front of the table, a paper held in his hands as he shook his head vigorously from side to side. A disgruntled face turned to Casey at the sound of her footsteps. "How could my own mother do this to me!" Mark's voice squeaked.

"What are you talking about?" Casey reached for the paper that he extended to her, while from the corner of her eye she saw Flint step into the room.

"Mrs. Grassick stopped in this noon," Flint explained even as Casey read the note left for them. "She offered to take your mother into Scottsbluff to the hospital to visit your father. She left that note explaining why she wouldn't be here for supper this evening."

"There's no way I'm going to eat my sister's

cooking!" Mark flopped into the kitchen chair. "I put up with it for an entire week when mom stayed with dad. It's a miracle I didn't die of ptomaine poisoning."

"Mark!" She couldn't stop the embarrassed flush from coloring her face as she glanced at Flint's amused expression. She also couldn't help noticing the way his rust-colored shirt matched the highlights in his brown hair and set off the pale tan of his slacks.

"I'm telling you, Flint, you've never met a worse cook in your life than Casey." She longed to reach over and jam her fist in Mark's mouth, anything to stop his humiliating words from tumbling out. "One time she tried to make some instant jello out of a box. She had to go and put too much water in it and we had to drink it!"

"I think we'd better change the subject, Mark," Flint said, his laughing eyes flicking over the enraged anger on Casey's face, "before you're forced to defend yourself. I'd already decided that rather than have your sister slave over a hot stove after she's worked so hard all day that we would all go into Fort Robinson and have a meal out tonight."

"Terrific!" Mark whooped.

"Does that suit you, Casey?"

For the first time in her life, Casey wished she could cook as well as her mother. After Mark's degrading statements she yearned to whip together some exotic meal. Instead she nodded stiffly. Mumbling quickly that she wanted to change, she escaped from the room before the hot tears of anger and humiliation could betray her.

During the entire journey to Fort Robinson, Casey was unbearably self-conscious. She tried to convince herself that it didn't really matter whether she could cook or not, but for the second time she found that it did. And she realized it did matter what Flint thought of her. Not even when the rolling Sand Hills gave way to the more spectacular scenery of the Pine Ridge region around Fort Robinson State Park did Casey's feeling of inadequacy abate. She found as she accepted Flint's hand when he helped her out of the car that she was uncomfortable. He was wearing a waist-length jacket in the same pale tan of his slacks with complementing stitching to match the rust brown of his shirt. His dress was so completely coordinated that the sporty denim material was overcome by the perfectly tailored appearance.

Casey found herself wishing that she had taken more care in choosing her own outfit. The white slacks and ruffled checked blouse did look nice, but she felt like a gauche country bumpkin. Too bad she couldn't have looked as good as Flint did, she sighed silently. At least she had forsaken her cowboy boots for her lone pair of white sandals.

As Mark led the way toward the one-time barracks complex for soldiers that had been turned

into a lodge and dining room for tourists, he immediately began informing Flint about the fort's history.

"That big white building there used to be the
post headquarters, but they use it for a museum
now. This was really a pretty famous fort, not just
during the settling of the west, but during the
world wars, too."

Casey knew that Mark had become enthralled
with the history of Fort Robinson over the years
and it really didn't matter to him whether Flint
was interested or not. He was going to hear about
it anyway.

"On the other side of the highway as we came
in," Mark continued, "is where Chief Crazy
Horse—you know, the one who was with Sitting
Bull at Custer's Last Stand—was killed resisting
soldiers who were trying to take him into a cell.
This is also where the Cheyenne Indians came led
by Dull Knife when they fled their reservation in
Oklahoma. When they refused to return to Oklahoma and were starved in an attempt to force them
to make the long trek back in the dead of winter,
they fought their way out of the Fort. Of course,
most people know all that stuff anyway." Mark
made a deprecating gesture with his hand.

"How do you turn him off?" Flint laughed
toward Casey as he held open the large door into
the Lodge.

"You don't. You wait for him to run out of gas."

Her glance at the sheepish expression on her brother's face was teasing and vengeful.

"Well, it was a pretty famous place," Mark defended himself while his long legs carried him into the lobby.

The trio had barely entered the dining room and seated themselves at a table when Mark was set upon by two blond-haired boys.

"Hey, Mark, we were just talking about you." The taller of the two thumped Mark soundly on the back.

"Kevin, Kyle!" Mark laughed as he tried to dodge a matching blow from the other one. "What are you doing here?"

"We convinced dad to take us to a movie since mom deserted us in favor of going to Scottsbluff." Casey had difficulty trying to figure out which one of the twin sons of Mrs. Grassick was speaking.

"She took my mom along leaving me at the mercy of my sister's cooking, until Flint rescued me." Mark's eyes sparkled with laughter.

"After you finish eating—or better yet, come and eat with us." The short one grabbed Mark's arm to pull him along and emphasize his invitation. "Dad's sitting right over there. We just ordered. Then you can come to the show with us later on tonight."

Mark glanced questioningly at Casey, the eagerness to join them glowing in his eyes.

"Go ahead," she nodded. "As long as Mr. Grassick doesn't mind running you home."

"He won't mind," the taller of the twins assured her.

The silence that followed the departure of the boisterous boys lasted through the first part of their meal. Despite her earlier anger toward her brother, Casey found herself wishing he was with them, anything to ease this silence that was making her so uncomfortable.

"You're very quiet tonight," Flint finally observed, his gray eyes studying the sudden flush in her cheeks. "I hope Mark's teasing hasn't upset you. Brothers are like that, you know."

"Of course it didn't. Why, he teases me like that all the time." The brief hesitation in her denial made it difficult for her to meet his gaze. "Besides, it's a well-known fact that I can't boil water."

"Can Smitty cook?"

"Smitty? How should I know?" This time her puzzled eyes met his squarely. "What has that got to do with it anyway?"

"From all I've heard, it's an accepted fact that you two are going to be married. It would be convenient if one of you could cook." One corner of his mouth slanted upward in obvious mockery.

"How quaint!" Casey retorted sarcastically. "If we were planning to get married, which we're not, it wouldn't be any of your business whether or not one of us can cook." She couldn't bear his teasing about her lack of culinary skill. It was an anger brought on by her own vulnerability that flamed through her words. "Tell me how you rate your girl friends on their cooking?"

"They're all capable of a good TV dinner." Flint's eyes crinkled into an audacious smile, though the rest of his expression was completely sober.

There was no doubt he was making fun of her short temper now, which only angered Casey further.

"No doubt a big he-man like you only attracts the feminine type." The smile on her face clashed with the fire in her dark eyes. "The ones with long hair and frilly white gowns. And of course, you have such broad shoulders for them to lean on."

"I think you're turning into a prickle poppy again."

"Well, if I am, it's your fault." Most of her anger subsided under the irresistible warmth of his smile.

"It's interesting to watch you when you get angry. Your face turns into a combination of snapping eyes and blushing cheeks, a most attractive combination."

That was the first compliment that Casey had ever received from Flint and it had the most disturbing effect on her pulse. She lowered her gaze to her empty plate, wishing she were some sophisticated person who could shrug off such an idle compliment with a witty remark.

"Let's take a walk around the Fort before going back to the ranch," Flint suggested, rising from the table and coming around to pull out Casey's chair.

She was too aware of her new reaction to him to do more than nod agreement. Waiting discreetly to one side as he paid for the evening meal, Casey noticed the glance of admiration the girl at the desk gave him. She couldn't help wondering what it would be like if they were on a real date together. Casey immediately tried to banish the thought, telling herself that a man like Flint would never be even slightly interested in a countrified girl like her. Still it was an exciting thought that wouldn't completely go away.

"Should we walk around the parade ground first?" Flint asked as they stopped on the wide veranda of the Lodge. At Casey's agreement, they descended the steps and walked toward the large oval surrounded by buildings.

The sun was pleasantly warm and the slight breeze carried the scent of freshly mown hay. There was little activity around the oval. Only at a distance could be heard the sounds of automobiles and tourists. At the near end of the parade ground was the present flagstaff, the American flag lifting gently in the wind.

As they walked slowly past the building housing the fire station, Casey spoke. "It's easy to imagine this side of the ground lined with cavalry barracks. Sometimes I can close my eyes and hear the call to 'boots and saddles.' "

"Mark was right about Fort Robinson. It's been an important post for over a hundred years." Their pace slowed as they rounded the oval near the commanding officer's quarters. Casey paused a moment.

"In a way, I hope a lot of people don't discover this place," she mused. "I don't really mind tourists coming to visit it and taking horseback rides along the trails once ridden by Red Cloud and Crazy Horse. I just don't want it becoming all commercialized. So much of the flavor of the old fort is still here that I wouldn't like it to change."

"American people are learning that there are some things that can't be exploited for their monetary value, but should remain unchanged so that future generations can appreciate their individual aesthetic value." Flint glanced down at Casey, a smile curving his mouth. "And that is as solemn as I'm going to get! It's a beautiful evening, an inspiring location, and most of the time, enjoyable company. I refuse to spoil them with discussions of the meaner side to the human race."

His hand rested on the back of her waistline with remarkable nonchalance, considering the havoc it wrought with her stomach as it turned upside down. Flint changed the subject, but Casey couldn't really concentrate on anything of any depth. She was too totally aware of him as a man.

CHAPTER EIGHT

CASEY HAD LEARNED A LOT about Flint that night during the walk around Fort Robinson and the long ride home. He had talked of his parents and grandparents, of his three brothers and one baby sister. For a time it had seemed they were growing closer, at least Casey felt that way. But their arrival at the Anchor Bar ranch had stifled that. A disgruntled Smitty was waiting for Casey, not hiding his disapproval of her accompanying Flint to dinner regardless of the fact that it had started out as a threesome. For the first time Casey had found herself resenting Smitty's possessive attitude.

To make matters worse, Flint had taken Smitty's ownership of Casey's company as fact and silently withdrew to his office. The evening that had been so pleasant ended on a sour note. At least it was true for Casey and Smitty, but she wasn't sure that Flint really cared one way or another.

She tried to force herself to accept the fact that she was probably no more than a diversion to him. What she had found hard to figure out the last three days since that night was what Flint meant to her.

That was the main reason Casey had ridden out
to Yucca Meadow alone. She wanted time to
rationalize her thoughts and put the recent events
in their proper perspective. Checking on the year's
new calves was a secondary motive. She nudged
Tally, her buckskin gelding, to the top of a small
bluff, halting him a few feet from the sheer drop to
gaze at the panorama of rolling hills. But the strug-
gles of a small red brown object below captured
her attention. The breeze carried a weak and plain-
tive cry.

Casey didn't need the pricked ears of her horse
to tell her that the cry had come from the same red
brown object. She turned her horse toward the
more sloping side of the bluff and let him pick his
own way down to the calf. All the while her eyes
scanned the surrounding hills looking for its mother. Casey knew of nothing more dangerous than a
cow protecting her offspring. Strangely enough
there wasn't another animal in sight. There was
one possible explanation—the calf had come from
a first-year cow whose maternal instincts hadn't
fully developed.

A hundred feet from the calf Casey halted her
horse. A rusted ring of barbed wire had become
twisted around its feet. The white stockings were
stained with bright red blood. Two coyotes
appeared mysteriously on a nearby hill. Casey
knew she didn't have much time to waste. The
darkened sand near the calf's legs and the lack of

any further struggle on his part told her clearly that the little tyke had lost a lot of blood. All she could do was free him from the wire and transport him back to the ranch house over the saddle of her horse.

The calf was too weak to resist as Casey dismounted and approached him, the wire cutters from her saddlebag in her hand. She knew she had nothing to fear from the coyotes since the presence of a human would keep them at a distance. Large, pain-filled brown eyes stared up at Casey as she quickly began snipping the barbed strands and gently unwrapping them from the calf's legs. She was careful to avoid the rusted prongs while silently wishing for the heavy leather gloves she had left on the kitchen counter. At last the calf was free, but he was too weak to do anything about it.

Casey struggled to manoever the heavy calf into her arms. He was like a dead weight when she finally managed to rise to her feet. Yet somewhere the calf found strength to emit one frightened cry. She had taken one step toward her horse, still standing where she had left him about fifty feet away, the reins dragging the ground, when she saw the buckskin's head turn toward the hill to Casey's left. The quick glance she cast occurred at the same time that a questioning bellow rang from the hill.

Casey's heart sank to her boot tops as she recognized the cow trotting purposefully down the hill.

There was only one cow in the whole Anchor Bar herd with long, twisting horns like that, a throwback to a distant strain of Texas longhorns that her father had used some years back when he was doing some experimental breeding. Crazy Woman, Mark had dubbed her. Even as Casey measured the distance between herself and her horse, she knew she didn't stand a chance of making it carrying the calf.

Yet, illogically, Casey hurried toward her horse, the calf still in her arms. Mingling in with the sound of the cow's hooves striding through the grass and sand came other sounds of creaking saddle leather and horse's hooves. From the corner of her eye, her heart leaping from fear into her throat, Casey saw the spotted rump of Flint's Appaloosa charging down the hill toward the cow. A rope snaked out from Flint's hand, a wide loop settling perfectly over the spreading horns, jerking the cow off her course toward Casey.

"The pickup and trailer are over by the west gate!" Flint shouted, his mount twisting and straining to keep the bucking and bellowing cow under control.

Casey didn't waste any time slinging the calf over her saddle, mounting and riding away. When she reached the pickup, she hurriedly fixed a place for the calf in the rear, lowered him gently into it and loaded her buckskin into the trailer. She had barely finished when Flint came galloping over the hill to join her.

His turbulent gray eyes rolled over her swiftly, the stormy havoc in his gaze doing nothing to improve the trembling that had weakened her knees. He sent his horse up the trailer ramp with a slap on the rump, locked the door in place and turned back to Casey. The savage expression on his face seemed to be set in stone, so harshly carved were the lines.

"I'll . . . I'll ride in the back with calf." Her voice rushed in to save her from the tempest that seemed to be brewing.

Flint crawled into the cab of the truck, slamming the door with frightful violence. The truck jumped into gear as it jolted its way over the rough road back to the ranch house.

"It'll be all right," Casey soothed, arranging the calf so that it lay partly on her lap. But she was trying more to comfort herself than the calf.

Sam Wolver, with his uncanny perception, met them at the main gate. He hopped into the rear bed of the pickup with Casey and began examining the wicked wounds on the calf's legs almost before the pickup ground to a halt. When Sam lifted the calf out of the truck, Casey hopped out to follow him. She wanted to be anywhere as long as it wasn't facing those unsettling gray eyes.

"Casey! I want to talk to you." Flint's voice was calm, but completely uncompromising.

"The . . . the calf." She motioned helplessly toward Sam, who was walking swiftly away.

"Sam can take care of it."

"Listen, Flint McCallister." The best defense was a good offense, Casey decided, drawing a deep breath as she plunged in. "I've just had a very unnerving experience and I'm not in the least interested in hearing any lectures from you. Right now I only want to be concerned about that calf. We can't afford to lose any of our stock."

"Now you listen, Casey Gilmore!" His hand shot out and jerked her arm back just as she was turning away. "Didn't you learn anything from your father's accident? Even he let someone know where he was going. If Sam hadn't seen you ride out that way, I would never have known where you were. Whatever prompted you to try to take that injured calf away from his mother alone?"

"In the first place, that calf was badly hurt." Her temper was slowly mounting and fighting back her initial trepidation. "And in the second place, that cow was nowhere in sight when I first got there. For all I knew it could have been a first-year calf. And in the third place—" Casey wrenched her arm away from him "—you don't have any right to tell me off!"

There was a breath of amusement in his voice and face at her sudden flare of temper. It frustrated her that he should find amusement in her anger.

"That's not the kind of language for a lady to use."

"I'm not a lady. I'm a prickle poppy, remember?" She tilted her head back to gaze defiantly at the gray eyes under the mocking, lifted brows.

"I'm beginning to wonder what's behind those thorns of yours," he murmured.

In one lithe, fluid movement his hands captured her waist and drew her to him as his mouth settled possessively over hers. In angry resistance, her hands moved to his chest to push herself away. Then the incredible warmth of his kiss swept through her, removing all thought of resistance, replacing it with an irresistible desire to respond. Casey felt her fingers curl into his shirt and the hard, muscular chest beneath it. A pulsating weakness spread through her body. She was drowning in a whirlpool of bliss and she wanted to savor every moment of it. Part of her was shocked by the almost total physical response his kiss was generating.

When his lips slowly lifted from hers, Casey was left in a state of supreme loss. She tried to swallow, to hold back the rising flood of breathlessness. His catalytic kiss had set off a fire, the flame of which was reflected in her eyes.

"I'd bet you've never kissed Smitty like that before." The words spoken by Flint's husky voice were like a pitcher of cold water to Casey.

"Why... why do you say that?"

"Because if you had, you'd either be married or having an affair. The first I know isn't true. And those innocent eyes of yours tell me quite clearly that the second isn't true either."

Casey stared up at his arrogantly sure eyes, feeling the shame that he should be able to know so completely about her. Oh, why did she have to react so wantonly to him? Her mind sobbed even as her eyes drank in the attractiveness of his face.

"You're lucky Smitty wasn't here to see what you just did," she retaliated.

"It takes two, Casey." Flint's gaze lazily rested on her still warm lips, softly swollen by his kiss. "I don't think anyone could believe that kiss was against your will."

She was impotent with frustration. The war of her conflicting emotions couldn't decide whether to melt into his arms or slap his face. So Casey did neither. She turned on her heel and escaped, a low throaty laugh of triumph dogging her feet.

IT WOULD NEVER DO, Casey scolded herself, to become attracted to Flint McCallister, worse yet to fall in love with him. That was exactly what was going to happen if she didn't watch her step. Sound advice, she decided even as she stared at him seated just a little in front of her in the family living room. Her throat tightened as she studied the way his auburn brown hair waved away from his forehead with careless perfection and the strong, chiseled lines of his profile like the sculpture of a Roman god. Inevitably her eyes were drawn to the sensuous curve of his mouth that had rocked the very foundation of her existence this afternoon.

"What do you think of the idea, Casey?" The knowing gray eyes turned toward her.

"I'm . . . sorry," she stammered. She had been concentrating so much on him that she didn't remember any words being spoken. "I didn't hear what you were saying."

His smile mocked her openly while his eyes twinkled over her flushed cheeks. "Your mother was just talking about the old-fashioned barn dance the Gordons are having Friday night. She said she wasn't going because John wasn't here. I suggested that she should go, that we could all go as a family."

"I really don't think I'd better." Lucille Gilmore looked up from the pile of socks in her lap. "You three can go by all means, but I wouldn't feel right going without John."

"Mother, you know you'd enjoy it." Casey shook her gaze free from Flint's hypnotic face. "Besides, how many of those dances have you been to where dad sat out every dance? He hates them, but he's never begrudged your going."

"The people who will be there are your friends and neighbors," Flint inserted. "No one will think unkindly of you accompanying your children, even if John is in the hospital."

"I'm sure they won't," Casey's mother agreed hesitantly. "But . . . ."

"No 'buts.' It's settled. We're all going," Flint said firmly. "We won't take 'no' for an answer, will we, Casey?"

She couldn't stop the tingle of pleasure at the coupling of her desires with his. Nor could she stop the glow from lighting her eyes as she agreed with him.

"You haven't made any arrangements to go to the dance with Smitty, have you, Casey? Because if you have...." Her mother spoke.

An uncomfortable twinge of conscience poked her as Casey tried to recall truthfully whether Smitty had mentioned it. "I'm sure he hasn't." The convincing tone was more for herself than for her mother. She accompanied the statement with a shy shrug of her shoulders. "He's become . . . too sure of himself lately, anyway."

Lucy Gilmore smiled at her, pleased at the suddenly feminine tactics her daughter seemed to be using. "All right, I'll go."

"Speak of the devil," Mark piped up, "here comes Smitty now."

Casey twisted from her chair, aware of the thoughtful gray eyes watching her.

"I'll go to the door," she offered unnecessarily, since Smitty came and went in their house as if it were his own.

"Hi, gorgeous," Smitty greeted her on the porch steps.

"Hi, yourself." She wished her sudden attack of nervousness would pass and that her smile would appear less forced than it was.

"You look a little pale. Are you feeling okay?"

"I'm fine." But her supposedly assuring laugh was jerky and unnatural.

Smitty's eyes narrowed on her face, not liking at all what he was thinking.

"I stopped to make sure about Friday night." He didn't like the color that washed over her face either.

"You are going with me?"

"To the Gordons?" Casey stalled. "We were just talking about it." She tried to smile into his questioning brown eyes. "Actually Flint and I just talked mom into going along. She didn't want to because of dad being in the hospital."

"Flint and you?" His gaze was diamond sharp.

"Does that mean you're going with him?"

"We're going as a family, Mark, mother, myself, and . . . and Flint." Why did she feel so guilty? It wasn't as if she had promised Smitty she'd go with him.

"Good old Flint's a part of the family now, is he?" There was no mistaking the sarcasm Smitty was directing at her now. "What am I? An old shoe you've thrown away?"

"You know you're welcome to come with us." Hurt dignity lifted her chin.

"No, thanks. Two's company; three's a crowd and all that rot!"

"Donald Smith! You have no right to talk to me like that!" Casey flared. "You don't own me! And just because I don't go to some party with you there's no reason for you to get so sarcastic."

"I don't mind you turning me down for your family, Casey. I just object to you turning me down for Flint McCallister. Johnny warned me about him, but I didn't think . . . . Oh, what's the use?"

"It isn't because of him at all." Her voice was low and trembling.

"Isn't it? It's written all over your face." Smitty stepped closer to her, his hands moving toward her only to fall at his side in despair. "When I think of how patient I've been with you! Casey, he isn't interested in you. He's been all over the world. What could he possibly see in a country girl like you?"

She wanted to put her hands over her ears and block out his hurting words. Everything Smitty was saying was true, things she had already told herself. The worst to bear was the fact that she had let Flint know that she was susceptible to his charms. What frightened her was how close was she from falling over the brink and tumbling into a love that would only bring her heartache.

CHAPTER NINE

CASEY WAS GLAD she was sitting in the back seat of the car and her mother was in front with Flint. Her tingling senses were all too aware of the confined space. The magnetic force that emanated from Flint was just as powerful as it had been all week, drawing her to him even when she wanted to stay away. Only the sensible side of her wanted to stay away while the wild, reckless side urged her ever closer. She felt like the child playing with matches who became fascinated by the flame. Her fear wasn't in getting burnt, but in being consumed by the fire.

Thinking about the evening ahead, Casey could not suppress a tide of exhilaration from sweeping over her. She knew at some point during the night that Flint would ask her to dance. She remembered the sensual warmth of his hands on her waist and the feel of his muscular body pressed against hers. No matter how hard she tried to deny that she shouldn't put herself in another vulnerable position, Casey knew she was going to accept him and thrill to every wonderful, rapturous moment of it.

The many petticoats under her red gold skirt rustled as she shifted position. Flint glanced over his shoulder at her. Under his smoky gaze, the last vestige of resistance melted away and Casey smiled at him.

"We're almost there," he said, as if needing to explain why he had turned to her.

Japanese lanterns were strung from pole to pole in the Gordons' back garden. Enormous sheets of plywood were stretched over the lawn to provide a dance floor. A hay wagon bordered one side serving as a platform for a local group of musicians. The combination of guitars, fiddles, accordion and drums filled the night air with a bouncing lively tune as Casey and Mark followed Flint and her mother from their car to the party area. Jim Kingston was at the microphone, his foot stomping to the beat of the drums while he called out to the dancers on the floor.

"Honor your partner, honor your corners. Now, an allemand left with the old left hand. On to the next with a right and left grand!"

On the outside of the dance floor, hands clapped automatically to the tune while bright, multicolored skirts whirled around the two squares. Flubbed directions were laughed off and dancers were pushed in the proper direction by more experienced dancers. Casey felt her toe tapping unconsciously. Her gaze strayed to Flint, who immediately smiled back.

"You like to dance." It was more a statement than a question.

"My one feminine characteristic." The gay atmosphere made her more bold than she had been and her brown eyes glittered up at him with laughter.

Her mother had been ensnared by Mrs. Gordon, and Mark had spotted Kevin and Kyle Grassick on the far side of the floor. Casey was left standing beside Flint, a situation she found very attractive, if a little dangerous.

"Was Smitty very upset that you didn't come to the party with him?" Flint's question was unexpected.

"Yes," she answered simply. She liked the way his eyes moved over her face, their smoky depths fanning the kindled fire inside her. "He blames you."

His gaze held her prisoner, frightening her a little by its intensity and exciting her at the same time. For a moment Casey felt dwarfed not just by his superior height but also by his nearly unlimited power over her to arouse a desire she hadn't even known she possessed.

"And he warned you about me." Flint spoke quietly, all the while studying her intently. "He told you I was more worldly and more experienced than you. That I could hurt you."

She nodded.

"It's true, Casey."

She blinked her eyes to hide the pain that stabbed her chest, before smiling broadly.

"So what! Surely in this modern age a woman's entitled to a dangerous interlude or two. After all, a man sows his wild oats before he finally settles down."

His throaty laughter was low and spellbinding.

"You're a trusting witch." The hand that touched her back sent a warm tongue of fire up her spine as Flint swept her on to the dance floor.

She didn't feel like a witch. She felt like the Sleeping Beauty awakened by a prince with dark auburn hair. Not even the glowering look from Smitty on the sidelines of the dance floor could prick the bubbling happiness that radiated from her face. Other men held her as her feet danced to the commands of the caller, but they were ghosts, shadowy beings that held none of Casey's attention.

The square ended amidst laughter and happy voices. Flint's hand retained its hold on Casey's, his smiling eyes glanced at her flushed cheeks. Other people, but mostly men, recognized him and walked over to make themselves known. Flint accepted their deferential attitudes while Casey marveled silently at his nearly regal bearing that still managed to convey midwestern friendliness. A gigantic swelling of pride filled her chest as ranchers' daughters glanced down at her hand held so securely by Flint, their eyes glinting enviously at her.

Brenda Fairlie, whom Casey hadn't seen since their high school days, was not the type to step back willingly from so small a claim to such a handsome man. She was tall and willowy fair. She walked toward Casey and Flint with a glowering Smitty in tow. Brenda had always seemed to be filled with her own self-importance even in schooldays—a sophisticated attitude that had kept Casey from attempting to make friends with her. Now, after almost three years at university, she almost reeked of class and culture.

"Casey, I've been going to stop and see you for just ages." Casey was forced to submit to a pathetically affectionate hug. "But you know how it is when you're home for only a few short weeks. You just can't see everyone. I was so glad when I heard the Gordons were having this party. It gives me a perfect opportunity to see everyone." Brenda fluttered her baby blue eyes at Flint. "You must be the new boss man from Ogallala. Smitty has been telling me about you, Mr. McCallister."

There was the barest flicker of concern in Casey's eyes as she watched Flint's amused glance sweep over Brenda's slender but shapely figure.

"My name's Brenda Fairlie." She introduced herself swiftly before Casey had an opportunity to do so. "Casey and I went to school together. Of course, my parents sent me on to university, so we haven't been very close since then."

She still manages to monopolize a conversation

and get her little gibes in, Casey thought cattily, hating the way Brenda was playing up so obviously to Flint.

Flint smiled. A mysterious humor lit his eyes. His hand tightened its hold on Casey's. "If you'll excuse us, I promised Casey the first polka."

Deftly and before a word of objection could be raised, he had Casey in his arms and on the dance floor. The look in his eyes plainly said, "This is our night." That was all it took for Casey to be lifted to a plateau that she had thought incapable of reaching. The mere thought that he had chosen her instead of someone as sophisticated and beautiful as Brenda, who seemed much more his type, made her head swim. Her feet didn't seem to touch the floor, time was suspended and the top of the world was below her feet. Casey wasn't even conscious of the music because the happy bubbling tune seemed to be coming from inside. The firm pressure of his arm around her waist had a burning warmth that brought a healthy glow of color to her cheeks. And his eyes held a promise that sent shivers of joy all through her. He whirled her through an intricate series of steps that she had never done before. But their harmony was complete and Casey never missed a move.

When the last note from the accordion faded away, they were on the far side of the floor, separated from the other guests. Casey was breathless, but from exhilaration and not exertion. The hand that had remained around her waist after the music stopped pushed her gently toward the darkness. Wanting to savor this moment of enchantment, she willingly succumbed to its pressure. Yet she couldn't meet his gaze for fear he would see how much more this moment meant to her than to him. A fence loomed before them and Casey raced to it gaily.

"Do you always sweep a girl off her feet like that?" The slight laughter that accompanied her question revealed a bit of her nervousness as she leaned against the whitewashed fence, her hands gripping the boards tightly. She felt as if she was floating and only by holding on tightly could she keep her feet on the ground.

"It's the best way to keep them from stepping on my feet," Flint smiled. His eyes captured hers for an instant before he removed a cigarette from his pocket. He offered one to Casey, but she declined, choosing instead to gaze at the heavens with its blue blanket filled with twinkling stars.

"I imagine you have a lot of them—girl friends, I mean." She glanced at him over her shoulder and silently wished his face wasn't in the shadows so she could see what he was thinking.

"Oh, they stand in line," he teased, leaning against the fence post so he could study her face.

"I'm sure mothers are always parading their daughters before you," Casey retorted, following his lead with the same amount of mockery in her voice. "You must be the most eligible bachelor in the territory, fair game for matchmakers everywhere."

"Are you contemplating throwing your hat in the ring with the others?" The tip of his cigarette glowed brightly as he inhaled.

"Me? I wouldn't be so presumptuous." It was difficult to laugh when he was looking at her through the gauzy veil of cigarette smoke. "I'm just a simple country girl, no competition compared to your other girls."

"You'd make a pretty good competitor."

Casey felt an absurd sensation of drowning as she gazed into the gray whirlpool of his eyes and listened to the seductive quality of his voice.

"Your eyes are dark and try very hard to hide a passionate nature. Your hair is soft and curling, free of sticky hairsprays so a man can touch it." As if to prove his point, a large hand reached out and ran its fingers through the curls before cupping the back of her head. She held her breath, her eyes closing briefly at the exquisite pleasure the intimate caress gave. "And your lips curve, soft and inviting, and are so very, very kissable." Her heart fluttered wildly. "And what's more—"

Flint didn't finish the sentence. He drew her slowly into his arms instead. She melted willingly against him, her back arching as his hold tightened around her waist. He kissed her with a thoroughness that left her weak and trembling.

"I frighten you, don't I?" Flint drawled.

Casey was frightened, frightened of the response he was capable of arousing because she couldn't control it. It was useless arguing the point when she knew her face mirrored her feelings all too clearly to him.

"I've never had an affair before." Her voice was husky.

"What a pity," Flint sighed. His eyes roamed intimately over her face, not bothering to mask the satisfaction on his own when he saw the radiant glow on her face.

"What is?" she asked breathlessly.

"You're twenty-one. In this modern age of liberated love, an affair would be the perfect answer." He rubbed her cheek with the back of his hand. Casey felt like nuzzling against it like a purring kitten. "But you're not the type, Casey, and you know it even though you say the words. You're the old-fashioned one-man kind, and that's rare these days."

She stood very still in his arms. His tender rejection stabbed at her heart.

"Do you always think you know women so well?" Casey lashed out in hurt anger.

A finger lifted her stiff chin with gentleness. His head was cocked slightly to one side as he studied the blackness of her eyes.

"I've been wrong before. But I'd be very disappointed if I were wrong about you." He moved away from her, holding out his hand for hers as he did so.

"We'll be missed at the party. I wouldn't want to incur any more of Smitty's wrath than I already have."

"Oh, we can't have that," Casey retorted sarcastically, refusing to take his hand.

"Prickle poppy," Flint whispered in her ear as he followed, closely behind her when she move hurriedly toward the lighted area.

In spite of herself, she did grin slightly, mollified by his teasing voice but sorely disappointed that he was ending their little game of love even though she tried to convince herself it was for the best. The yearning emptiness was still inside her, aching to be filled. A little voice inside asked why she couldn't have spent a few more minutes in his arms.

"Ah, Smitty," Flint's voice echoed clearly through the music. "We were just talking about you."

"I can just bet you were." Smitty glared angrily at Casey. "I've been looking for you."

"Have you?" she retorted defiantly. "What happened to darling Brenda? I'm surprised you were able to tear yourself away from her."

"Excuse me, Casey." And Flint slipped away. She couldn't help staring after him.

"Oh, boy, is he setting you up for the kill!" Smitty exclaimed as he looked at the forlorn expression on her face.

"Would you like to dance with me? Because if

you don't, you can just leave!" What a relief it was
to turn her frustrated anger on someone other than
herself.

CHAPTER TEN

THAT EVENING HAUNTED CASEY for days. Except for that one incident with Smitty, Flint had been exceptionally attentive the rest of the evening but only in a crowd. Never again did he try to be with her alone and never in the days that followed. Casey felt he was trying to shut her out of his life.

If only she were sophisticated and capable of carrying off an affair with aplomb, she thought. Then she laughed bitterly that such an idea would even cross her mind. Flint had been very correct when he said she wasn't the type. That didn't compensate for the fact that an affair would be the only romance that Flint would offer. His worldliness and wealth excluded her from entering any race where the stakes were marriage.

Casey tossed a pebble in the water, watching the waves circling out from where the stone hit. A glance from Flint could send the same ripples through her body, but with a more violent reaction. The physical and emotional demands of her body had suddenly come of age. It was becoming apparent that her love for Flint couldn't be denied any more than her desire could. And her love for him grew daily.

She tried desperately to ignore the weeks ahead, because it was such a short time until her father would be home and Flint would be leaving. Once she had looked forward to that day. Now she could feel just a small amount of the hollowness his departure would bring. It was a void, a black ominous pit that yawned ahead of her. If the thought could depress her so much while he was still here, what would it be like when he had really gone?

A drop of water fell on her arm as the ground suddenly vibrated around. Her gaze left the pool in front of her, turning upward to the sky. A jagged fork of lightning pierced through dark, rolling clouds. When Casey had ridden out to the small lake, she had noticed these same clouds hovering near the western horizon. Now they completely blackened the sky. A growl of thunder shook the ground again as another drop of rain fell on her. These sudden storms were common in Nebraska. She glanced toward the grassy area where her buckskin had been grazing.

His head was up, his eyes rolling in fear at the golden white spears of lightning falling out of the thunderclouds. An enormous clap of thunder sent the horse crouching on all four legs before he seemed to explode away from the lake. Casey leaped to her feet, shouting at the horse already racing away, his head held high and to one side to keep the trailing reins from entangling in his feet.

"Tally! Tally!" But her call was muffled by the onslaught of rain that the black clouds set free.

In seconds she was soaked to the skin. There was no use standing here staring after the fleeing horse, Casey decided disgustedly. She stalked to the top of the hill, but the buckskin was nearly out of sight. In angry desperation she placed two fingers in her mouth and whistled shrilly for him. It was useless. The horse didn't even slow up for two strides. She glanced irritatedly at the dark clouds before setting off at a walk toward the ranch house nearly seven miles away. If only she had stopped feeling sorry for herself long enough to look up to the sky, she wouldn't have been in this mess, she told herself disgustedly. Her toes were already beginning to squish in her boots.

A questioning whinny halted her feet. The corners of her mouth curved upward in a hopeful smile. Maybe Tally had come back. But when she stared ahead of her, Casey saw a white horse making his way toward her.

"Mercury, how's the old boy today?" Her voice was a soothing caress as the horse nuzzled her face. "No sugar, feller."

Lightning flashed again, this time much closer as the violent storm moved in with all its intensity. Casey knew she had one chance of making it to the house before the full force of the storm descended on her. But she hadn't ridden Mercury for several years. It was a question of whether she'd be able to control him and direct him to the ranch with just knee signals. She had no choice; she had to give it a try.

The white horse was startled when she pulled herself onto his back. He moved restlessly beneath her while Casey spoke to him in a soothing and reassuring voice before urging him forward. He stepped out hesitantly, slowly accustoming himself to the weight on his back that he hadn't felt for years. But memories and habits are quickly recalled. Soon Casey had him in an easy canter, the aging white horse responding to the slightest pressure as when he was young and he and Casey were inseparable.

The rain fell harder, the drops becoming stinging pellets on exposed skin. The ground vibrated beneath the horse's hooves from the rolling thunder while the sky was alternated between lightness and dark by the lightning bolts. Mercury lengthened his stride until he was at a full gallop. It happened so gradually that Casey wasn't even aware of it until she noticed the ground racing past them at a faster speed.

She had no means to slacken his pace and it was all she could do to grip his rain-soaked sides with her wet legs. Her heart was pounding in her throat as they raced full speed over the Sand Hills. Casey knew she should slow him down, that the pace was too much for a horse his age carrying her unaccustomed weight. But she, perhaps like the horse, was remembering other times when Mercury was younger and they had ridden like this over the prairie. She kept telling herself that he wasn't laboring a bit, that his stride was just as effortless as it had always been.

Just as the thought crossed her mind, Casey felt a slight difference in the rhythm of his gait. Two strides before Mercury went down, Casey knew he was falling. She jumped free just as he somersaulted through the air, head over heels. A thick yucca bush broke her fall although she lay on the ground with the wind knocked out of her. She mentally checked her body to make sure she had no broken bones. Then her dark eyes turned toward the inert white form a few feet away. A mixture of rain and mud had marred the pure whiteness. She stumbled and crawled to the horse. Her eyes filled with tears as she knelt beside the huge chest that had been drinking in large quantities of air just moments before. Now it was still.

"Mercury?"

Her hand reached out to touch the white forelock. Her whole body was shaking with the realization that her horse was dead. Sobbing openly now, Casey gathered the white head onto her lap, the gazelle-soft eyes now shut in death.

"I'm so sorry." The shaking, whispering voice was barely audible as she buried her head in the horse's neck. Her dearest possession and friend was gone. The lightning, the thunder, the rain, they didn't matter any more.

She was barely conscious of the rain subsiding and finally ceasing altogether. Not until two hands

gripped her shoulders was Casey's mind drawn
from the horse in her arms. Her misty gaze looked
up at the sympathetic gray eyes below the wet hat
brim.

"Your buckskin came back to the ranch. I was
worried," was all Flint said as he pressed a willing
Casey against his broad chest where she sobbed
anew.

"I ... I ... w-was riding h-him. H-He started running and . . . and I cou-couldn't stop him." The
stranglehold on her throat made her explanation
difficult, but the comforting circle of his arms
made her want to talk. "Then he . . . he fell. He's
dead, Flint." This time Casey looked into his face.

Flint smoothed the curls of brown hair away
from her cheek. "Don't blame yourself, Casey.
Isn't it better this way?" His smile was so gentle. "I
bet he's still running on into heaven, free forever."

The whimsical thought brought more solace to
Casey than any logical argument she had considered. Remembering the way they had been racing
over the hills before he had fallen made it an all
the more cherished thought. She rested her head
on his shoulder, the pain in her heart easing.

When his lips touched her hair, she couldn't help
moving closer against him, snuggling into the comfortable warmth of his arms. She felt Flint's lips
touch her forehead and the quivering sensation
race clear down to her feet. Then they brushed the
wetness of her eyelashes, the bridge of her nose,

seeming to take time to touch each pale freckle on her face. His hand bit into her shoulder as he whispered her name so softly.

Her lashes fluttered open to gaze into the smoky fire of his eyes while she tilted her head upward to receive his kiss. Without conscious direction her hand reached up and removed his hat just before his mouth claimed hers. Then the other hand joined the first, curling into the silkiness of his hair, drawing him closer to her. Waves of ectasy washed through her, each one leaving her weaker and more pliable than the one before. The warm moisture of his mouth drowned any resistance. At the increased demand in his kiss, her lips parted involuntarily, bringing her a new rapture in unearthly enjoyment. His arms were steel bands that pressed her tightly against him until every button on his jacket was driven through the thin cotton of her blouse.

His lips left hers as Flint buried his head in the curve of her neck, nibbling at the sensitive cord until Casey moaned from the pleasure the action invoked. Now Casey could feel the rapid beat of his heart through his shirt as it marked time with the erratic pace of hers. An exquisite quiver of satisfaction claimed her as she realized that she had aroused him as thoroughly as he had aroused her.

Flint returned his lips once more to her mouth, roughly and possessively, as their physical desire mounted to an even higher pitch. But suddenly she experienced fear. Her lips became still beneath his mouth. Without being aware that she had reached any decision, she began struggling to free herself from the male body pressing down on her. A pleading "no" was whispered out of the corner of her lips. At first Flint ignored her, increasing the ardor and passion in his kiss until he almost took her breath away. Casey tried not to respond, but she did, although the fact that she was fighting it showed through.

In the next instant the heat of his body was taken away from her and a heavy-breathing Flint was towering above her. Casey knew the flush of her passion was still on her face and her lips were swollen from his kisses. And the flame of desire still burned brightly in his eyes, too. He stared silently down at her for a moment, then turned away. She opened her mouth to speak, but Flint silenced her.

"Don't apologize." Flint grasped her roughly by the shoulders, forcing her to look into his face. "If . . . . You wouldn't have been able to stop me, Casey, and we both know it."

Anger was in his voice and face. Casey felt a certain amount of humiliation at the fact that it was directed at himself and not at her. Plus she knew that another few minutes under the expertise of his lovemaking and she wasn't sure she would have tried to resist.

"Take my horse and ride back to the ranch,"

Flint ordered crisply. "Send Sam out so he can help me bury Mercury."

Casey glanced at the white body, then up to the thinning gray clouds overhead. Unwillingly she thought it had been one of these violent storms so common to the Nebraska sand hills. One minute the sky was clear and in the next it was covered by rolling thunderheads. Just as quickly, the storm passed, sometimes leaving destruction and devastation in its wake. She glanced at Flint and the hard, stonelike expression on his face. Was he like one of their storms? Arriving unexpectedly, destroying the peaceful routine of the ranch and Casey, then departing just as swiftly?

Her gaze returned to Mercury. "Something dies and something is born." But hadn't the love that had been born between her and Flint been just as quickly killed? What was to be born in its place? Heartbreak?

Poor Mercury, she mused silently, *how lucky you are to be free*. Then she mounted Flint's Appaloosa and rode off.

CHAPTER ELEVEN

THE AFTERNOON WAS UNBEARABLY HOT. Not even a blade of grass was stirring. The western sun was a searing ball of flame scorching the sandy earth. Casey was depressed and irritable, a condition that had become very prevalent the last two days. Her irritation had been compounded today by her visit to the Smith ranch. She had gone to make arrangements to use their plane the following day to check fences in the far sections. Unfortunately, as far as Casey was concerned, the entire family was on the porch when she arrived at the Bar S.

Smitty's parents greeted her with their usual enthusiasm, insisting that she sit with them and have a glass of tea. Smitty's moody silence had been so marked that it was impossible for his parents not to notice. When he finally did speak, his sarcastic inquiries about "McCallister" had brought startled looks from his parents and questioning glances at Casey's grim expression. Casey had tried her best to keep her replies civil, but occasionally her own short temper crept through. Mr. and Mrs. Smith had nervously laughed off some of the more pointed barbs exchanged between Casey and Smitty, trying to treat the animosity between the pair as a lovers' quarrel.

Yet it was when Mr. Smith had jokingly said to Smitty, "Well, it's Friday night. I suppose you're going to be taking the car tonight and spiriting Casey off to some movie," that the barely disguised show of politeness had vanished.

"I'm sure Casey and McCallister have other plans for this evening," Smitty had retorted sharply. "But I will be needing the car." He had glowered at Casey triumphantly. "I thought I'd stop over to the Fairlie place and see Brenda."

Casey had muttered the first excuse that had popped into her head and had left. It had become vastly immaterial whether or not the plane was to be borrowed the following day or not at all. First Flint had practically turned his back on her, treating her as if she were poison ivy that he shouldn't get close to, and now Smitty was deserting her as well for that ridiculous chit of a girl Brenda Fairlie. Casey was so horribly mixed up that nothing seemed to make any sense any more.

Part of the problem with Flint was her own making. She had difficulty meeting his eyes squarely. A mixture of shame and elation washed over her when he walked into a room where she was. She was so confused that she didn't know if she was supposed to ignore what had happened between them or what. But Flint's clipped words whenever he did speak to her had implied that was the direction she was to take.

A huge blowfly buzzed noisily around her ear. She swatted at it uselessly as she continued toward the house. In a fit of pique Casey slammed the screen door shut behind her as she entered the kitchen. The room was strangely empty. At this time of the afternoon it was usual for her mother to be in the kitchen preparing the evening meal. Casey shrugged away her slight uneasiness and removed the pitcher of iced tea from the refrigerator. A glance at the stove told her that nothing was even on it in anticipation of dinner.

She had just poured herself a glass of tea and was raising it to her lips when she heard a sound from the doorway. She glanced back, expecting to see her mother enter the room, but instead she saw Flint. He was rubbing the back of his neck in a gesture of tiredness. He was studying Casey with an abstracted thoughtfulness. There was a strained, hard look in his expression and weariness in his eyes. She stifled a desire to rush over and comfort him, choosing instead to keep her back to him.

"I've spent half the day looking for you." The sharp edge of his voice slashed her already frayed nerves. Luckily her back was to him and he couldn't see her flinch. "Won't you ever learn to let someone know where you're going?"

"I didn't think it mattered," Casey flashed back just as sharply. "Where's mom?"

"The next time, don't think, just do as you're

told." It hurt terribly to have Flint speak to her as if she were a child. "As for your mother, the hospital called this morning—"

"Is dad coming home?" She made her voice appear eager even though she knew such an event would mean Flint's departure.

"No."

The decisive word forced Casey to swallow a lump of apprehension as she waited expectantly for an explanation. Flint studied her grimly before continuing.

"He contracted a virus of some sort. Your mother went in this morning because the doctor felt his condition was critical."

The quick gasp for air didn't ease the sudden knotting of her stomach muscles. Casey wanted Flint to stay, but not at the expense of her father's health. Out of the hardness of his face, Flint spared her a sympathetic glance.

"Lucille called just a few minutes ago saying he had improved considerably," he reassured her. "I've convinced her that right now her place is with your father, so she's staying in Scottsbluff with her sister until he's released from the hospital."

Flint crossed the room and poured himself a glass of tea while Casey stared at him silently. She was trying to adjust to the sudden news and the unusual tension that seemed to possess Flint. She had studied him so often these past weeks that she could tell there was something more he wanted to say. He studied the brown liquid in the glass before he bolted it down as if it were hard liquor. Then he turned his bland gray eyes to her.

"I called my sister this morning." He paused, examining Casey's face. "I've made arrangements for you to stay with her until your mother and father come home."

"What!" Casey was flabbergasted. "What are you talking about?"

There was just enough outraged anger in her question to bring a tightening of Flint's jaw as he set the glass on the counter.

"I've already discussed it with your mother and she agrees with me that you shouldn't stay here on the ranch with an unmarried man in the same house, namely me."

"What about Mark? He's here."

"A fifteen-year-old boy is hardly a suitable chaperon."

"This is preposterous! I feel like some Spanish girl that has to be kept under lock and key!" She shook her head in disbelief.

Before the anger in Flint's eyes could be voiced, she rushed in, more calmly this time. "You can just call your sister back and tell her I'm not coming. My place is here at the ranch. There's too much work to be done for you to do it alone."

His hand exploded on the countertop, the violence causing her to jump.

"Casey, can't you get it through your head that I don't want you here!"

It was as if his hand had knocked all the wind out of her as she stared blindly at the uncompromising gray eyes. Their cold hardness froze her as effectively as their fire had once burned her.

Casey turned away, her vision blurred with tears. She was certainly left in no doubt of his feelings toward her. If he had drawn her a picture it couldn't have been any plainer. He was tired of her. Well, Casey thought, gathering herself together, she had some pride left, too.

"I'll go." The admission of defeat was hidden in her calm voice.

She heard Flint sigh behind her, but it wasn't a sigh of relief but of exasperation and irritation. His hands gripped her shoulders and turned her to face him. Casey rigidly controlled her muscles so they wouldn't react the way they wanted to and move into his arms and against the broad, inviting chest.

"I've handled this badly." Flint seemed to be choosing his words with care, trying to appear logical and in control. But the muscle at the side of his jaw was twitching.

"What I'm trying to get at is that there have been some things happening between us." His eyes bored into hers, willing her to make it easier. But Casey remained stiff and unyielding, her gaze cold and challenging. Her lack of cooperation angered him. "If we were here alone . . . ." He stopped. Casey raised her eyebrow in what she felt was mocking amusement.

"To put it bluntly, I think you've fallen in love with me," Flint stated. His grim and forbidding expression brought a faint flush of humiliation to Casey. Why did her emotions have to be so transparent to him?

"Of all the egotistical men I've ever met—" Casey fought to keep her voice as cold and biting as she could and not let her trembling body take over "—you beat them all! Have you become so used to women falling all over themselves to get near you that you expect it as your due? With your arrogance, I suppose you think that one little kiss and a girl is yours." She paused to take a deep breath. "Well, let me tell you one thing, Flint McCallister, this little gal isn't one of them. All along I knew you were a despicable man. I played along with you for a while because I wanted to find out what your game was. So don't bother to add me to your list of conquests."

"Are you telling me the truth? Because if you're not, I'll—" His fingers were like ten separate vices gripping her shoulders. She stared up at him haughtily, mocking his attempt to get the real truth out of her.

"What do you think?" she retorted sarcastically. "If you'll just let go of me, I'll go and pack. It should be fun enlightening your sister about her big brother."

"Go!" Flint uttered hoarsely, releasing her abruptly. "Get out of here!"

"With pleasure," she answered with equal venom.

Nearly three hours later Flint and Casey arrived at the hospital. John Gilmore looked considerably weaker, but he still managed to jest to his daughter that he had to enter the hospital to get sick. Casey was surprised that she could appear so natural and relaxed in front of her parents. Inside her body was a turmoil of pain and rejection that should have numbed her from any feeling. She avoided any reference to the grim Flint McCallister who stood silently in the room. He had barely said five words to John Gilmore before moving to a wall where he could lean back and stare at Casey.

There was a moment when Casey had to meet her father's questioning eyes after her mother had mentioned that Casey was going to stay with Flint's sister. But she somehow managed to make light of it.

"Now how do you like that, dad?" she had laughed. "You always said there was a silver lining to every cloud. Here you are in the hospital and I'm going on a vacation!"

Her mother cast an apprehensive glance at Casey then over to Flint. Although her daughter seemed natural, Flint didn't. No mother could have been unaware of the undercurrents that had been flowing around her house the last two weeks. Perhaps she had made a mistake agreeing with Flint's suggestion that Casey stay with his sister. It had seemed a sensible solution at the time. Just as she was about to make an excuse to see her daughter alone and find out what difficulties, if any, existed between Casey and Flint, one of the doctors stopped in for a late check on his patient. Flint took the opportunity to recommend that he and Casey leave. The strain of wearing the heavy mask of gaiety was getting to be too much for Casey, so she agreed quickly. She paused long enough to assure her father that she would be up to see him as often as she could.

Casey never realized the journey from Scottsbluff to Ogallala could seem so long. Nor did she ever think that Flint could treat her so disdainfully. Even the arch of his eyebrow when he turned in her direction, which was seldom, seemed to look at her with displeasure above the stone coldness of his eyes. As for herself, she didn't attempt to inject any warmth into the car. She huddled against the car door and stared out the window, trying to make believe that Flint wasn't there at all.

When they passed Chimney Rock, painted a fiery orange by the late setting sun, Casey felt the long stifled tears cloud in her eyes. Gazing at the inverted funnel formation of rock, a famous landmark on the way west, made her wonder what tormenting hardships were ahead of her. She had come to acknowledge her love for Flint as genuine and the realization that he didn't want her was nearly a fatal wound, one that her pride would never let show.

The dark waters of Lake McConaughy blinked at them from behind the sandy bluffs that rimmed the Platte River Valley. Casey found herself wondering more and more about her final destination. She discovered that she knew very little about the woman she was going to stay with other than her name, Gabrielle, her age, twenty-four, and her occupation, a freelance writer. She longed to ask Flint questions, but each impulse to do so was pushed back. Feeling as she did for him, it was wrong for her to become involved with his family. How many endless days would stretch ahead where she would picture him with them? A bitter, ironic smile teased her lips as she remembered saying to her father that this was going to be a vacation. That was far from the truth. It was going to be a test of her nerves. Right now she didn't think she could stand up under it.

Flint turned the station wagon off the main road toward the lake and continued along a dirt road until he reached a group of lake-front cabins. In the waning purple of the evening light, Casey's eye was caught by the modernistic, chalet-type cabin with a wide veranda-like porch at the rear of the structure looking out over the shimmering waters. The simplistic design reeked of class and distinction, which was probably the reason Casey shuddered when Flint pulled into its narrow drive. The affluence it represented intimidated her and made her more aware of the mediocrity of her background.

The car rolled to a halt at almost the same pace that her heart slowed its beat. Flint turned off the motor. Casey waited expectantly for him to open the door and signal the end of the journey, but he waited. In the dimness of their confines, she saw him turn toward her. The focus of his attention quickened her impulse. The distance between them seemed so small that with just the slightest effort she could be in his arms. It was surprising how cold she suddenly felt inside, and she remembered vividly the feel of his warm body against hers.

"You said at the hospital that you were going on a vacation." The urgent compassion in his voice grated at Casey as no amount of anger could have. She didn't want his pity. "I hope you meant that. Too many things have happened in a few short weeks. A slower pace will help you think things through, give you a chance to discover your true feelings about things."

"Stop the pretense," she answered bitterly. "You know I only said that to reassure my father. Save the pity for the poor girls who fall for male chauvinist egomaniacs like you!"

For a moment anger flared blackly in his eyes before the gray hardness returned. "Common sense should make you admit that what I'm saying is right."

"Common sense told me that I never should have let you set foot on the Anchor Bar. The biggest mistake I ever made was not listening to it." This denial of him was the only defense she had.

"You're making an even bigger mistake if you keep pushing me," Flint warned, ominously leaning closer.

"Conversation with you is pointless," Casey replied scathingly, unwilling to admit that she was slightly intimidated by his threat. She pushed open her door and stepped out before he had a chance to stop her.

Her legs felt like liquid jelly beneath her, but she managed to gaze haughtily at him as he slammed his car door shut and removed her suitcases from the back. The contemptuous disdain in his face brought a strangling lump to her throat. All she wanted was to be away from him, to indulge herself in the tears that she had fought all afternoon. She didn't want to give him the satisfaction of knowing he could make her cry. Flint signaled for her to precede him to the cabin. It was difficult to keep her back straight, her chin up and her pace slow with his steady gaze on her back. Relief washed over her as the front door opened and she was bathed in the light.

"I was beginning to think you weren't coming!" the tall, dark-haired girl in the doorway called out in a happy, welcoming voice.

CHAPTER TWELVE

"HE WAS TERRIBLY ABRUPT, wasn't he?" Gabrielle, or Gabbie as she had insisted that Casey call her, commented after Flint had left. "Hardly the epitome of male courtesy?"

"Yes, he was very sharp," Casey willingly admitted, glad that someone else had noticed his cold indifference.

Flint had been almost embarrassingly short, making only the briefest of introductions before setting the suitcases down and stating that he had to leave to make it back to the ranch. Gabbie's offer for refreshments had been brushed aside. He had left with only a curt nod to Casey which was supposed to serve as goodbye.

Although Casey was still uneasy, Gabbie's handshake had been warm and friendly. Even now she was obviously trying to establish some degree of comradeship between them. The trouble was that Casey had discovered that the sudden departure of Flint had removed her protective armor. The rigidity and tenseness were gone and she was dangerously close to tears.

"I have some cold drinks in the kitchen. Why

don't you go on into the living room and make yourself comfortable?" Gabbie suggested.

Casey glanced appreciatively at the tall girl with long, straight dark hair.

"Thanks, I will," she agreed.

The room was cool and cheerful, but Casey wasn't in the mood to appreciate it. The walls were white with large, darkly stained beams giving it an elegantly rustic atmosphere. An enormous white wicker chair offered its cocoonlike shelter to her and Casey allowed herself to be lost in its brightly flowered cushions. Here restless hands played with the large fern plant in the cedar pot beside her chair. Gabbie joined her only a few minutes later, handing her a tall glass already gathering moisture on the outside.

"I'd better warn you I put some vodka in that," Gabbie told her as Casey lifted the drink to her mouth.

The citrus taste of juice felt refreshing to her dry throat, while the more potent liquor relaxed her muscles and warmed the hollows inside.

"You looked in need of something stiffening," Gabbie added.

"I was," Casey sighed. She stared at the glass, listening to the sound of the ice clinking against the side.

"How's your father?" Gabbie curled her long frame onto the brilliant Prussian blue sofa.

"Much better. I guess the virus had reached its

peak this morning. He was joking a bit this evening when Fl—I was there." Casey's mind was racing to think of anything to say, anything to keep her mind from returning to those thoughts of Flint.

"Flint seemed terribly concerned when he called me this noon." Gabbie's blue green eyes studied Casey thoughtfully before returning to the large silver bracelet on her wrist. "He isn't the type to cry wolf without a reason."

Casey swallowed hard, but she couldn't get rid of the lump in her throat. Gabbie paused just long enough to give Casey an opportunity to comment if she wanted before she continued.

"The few weekends that Flint has been back, he's told us quite a lot about your family. He admires your parents. You have two brothers, don't you?"

Casey nodded that she did.

"Flint thinks that Mark—he's the youngest, isn't he—will make a fine rancher. Flint said he had a natural feel for the land."

Flint! Flint! Flint! There was no escape from him. Tears welled in her eyes. In another moment they would be running down her cheeks. Casey jumped to her feet, placing the glass haphazardly on the glass coffee table.

"You'll have to excuse me." Casey fought for composure. She refused to cry in front of Flint's sister. "I know it's early yet, but I'd really like to—"she swallowed back a sob"—to turn in. This morning seems as if it has gone on for a whole week."

"You don't have to make any excuses," Gabbie smiled, rising to her feet as well. "I understand."

She led Casey to a small bedroom in the rear of the cabin, showed her where the bathroom was, the empty drawers in the bureau and the closet for her clothes before taking leave.

"Stay in bed as late as you like. I work in the mornings, so just cover your head with a pillow when you hear the typewriter. Have a nice night, Casey."

As the door closed behind the tall dark-haired girl, Casey sank on to the single bed. She forced herself to remove her shoes, tights, dress and slip before she leaned back on the bed and stared at the ceiling. Then the textured paint was obscured by a wall of tears.

IT TOOK CASEY nearly a half hour the following morning to repair the ravages wrought by last night's storm of tears. Even then no artificial means could restore the lack of color in her cheeks and the dullness in her eyes. Shrugging that it didn't really matter what she looked like any more, Casey pulled a pale green top over her head to match the faded green cut-off jeans. Just as she entered the living room, Gabbie walked out of the kitchen carrying a tray.

"Break time for breakfast," she announced gaily, walking on past Casey toward the glass door that led onto the veranda. "I always say that when I have a particularly bad morning at the typewriter. Any excuse to get me away from that monster! Toasted muffins, jam and coffee—how does that sound to you?"

"It sounds good." Casey followed her onto the wide porch. She couldn't help admiring the sea-green kimono Gabbie was wearing, her long dark hair piled on top of her head.

"Like the outfit?" Gabbie questioned at Casey's prolonged inspection. "Most people expect writers to be slightly eccentric and bizarre. I don't like to disappoint them."

"You look so natural wearing that I can't imagine anyone regarding it as bizarre." Casey smiled as she pulled a chair away from the wrought-iron table. "What's it like being a writer?"

"It has its peaks and valleys. The valleys seem exceptionally deep when you're staring at an empty sheet of paper and the typewriter keys are staring back. But it's the supreme ego trip when you see your name below a published article, if— capital letters, IF—you don't let yourself get weighted down by rejection slips."

Casey sipped carefully at the scalding cup of coffee, inhaling the aroma at the same time. "What kind of things do you write exactly?" she asked as she spread blackberry jam on a muffin.

"Short stories, magazine articles," Gabbie's

hand trailed off into space suggestively. "The Great American Novel is waltzing around in my head, but so far it hasn't danced itself onto paper." She leaned back in her chair, nibbled at her muffin and gazed out at the blue waters of the lake.

The blood drained away from Casey's face as the aristocratic profile stood out against the backdrop of blue sky. It was startling to see how this modellike girl looked so much like Flint. Gabbie had the same strong cheekbones, straight nose and high arched brows. Her jawline was more refined and feminine. She was strikingly beautiful in her own individualistic way. But now she was a constant reminder of Flint's unnerving handsomeness.

"Did you find the family resemblance?" A pair of blue green eyes stared back into the pain-filled brown ones. Their knowing look was extremely difficult to meet.

"I . . . I don't know wh-what you mean," Casey stammered, trying to ignore Gabbie's direct gaze.

"All of us McCallisters look alike in some way or another. Flint and I have almost the same bone structure, although my hair is darker than his and I don't have those darling creases that give his mouth a permanent smile. You were bound to notice the resemblance sooner or later," Gabbie replied blandly.

Casey made an attempt to hide her confusion behind her coffee cup as she admitted that there was a slight resemblance.

"You look as if you've spent the night crying."

Casey couldn't stop the cup from clattering back to its saucer at Gabbie's pointed remark.

"I didn't get nicknamed Gabbie just because my first name is Gabrielle and I didn't become a moderately successful writer by not observing the people around me. I'm not a subtle person and I'm not going to pretend to be one." Her eyes softened as she watched the conflicting emotions race across Casey's face. "I'll wager those tears last night were over my brother and not your father. Am I right?"

Casey stared at her aghast. How could Gabbie possibly know? How could she possibly guess? She opened her mouth to deny the charge vehemently, but instead an almost incoherent "yes" tumbled out.

"Do you want to tell me about it?" Gabbie coaxed her gently.

Casey raised her lowered head and gazed at her thoughtfully.

"I talk a lot, but I don't betray a confidence, so you don't have to worry that I'll go carrying tales to Flint," Gabbie assured her. "If you'd rather not tell me, that's all right too."

The need to lighten her burden by talking was overwhelming. Besides, there was something about Gabbie, just as there had been about Flint, that told Casey she could trust her. But there was also a certain point beyond which Casey wasn't going to confide. She held back the more intimate details, relating only the briefest of outlines to Gabbie, ending with, "He made it very clear he didn't want me."

The composure with which she retold the story surprised her. The words seemed to have come out of another person. Perhaps, she decided, she had cried out all her tears last night and no emotions remained.

"The unfeeling brute!" Smoke from her recently lit cigarette puffed expressively from Gabbie's pink-tinted lips. "Even if he is my brother, that was a terribly callous thing to do." The glimmering green of her dress was reflected in the gleam of her eye. "If Flint was so blind not to see what a gem she could have had, then he deserves whatever comes next."

"What are you talking about?" Casey was just a little bit puzzled by Gabbie's cryptic remark.

"Just generalities." Gabbie shrugged, rising from her chair. "I have to get back to work. You're welcome to take a swim if you like. The beaches here are absolutely gorgeous."

Minutes after Gabbie left, Casey heard the tapping of a typewriter. She sighed heavily, wishing she were back at the ranch where she could have at least busied herself with work. Now all she had to do was to gaze at the beauty of the lake, its sandy beaches stretching out their golden fingers to the sky-blue water. Amidst all this splendour of sun and sand, Casey was only conscious of her aching love for Flint. His face danced before her with almost jeering vividness.

The jangling ring of the telephone in the house startled her momentarily as if it were an alarm clock ringing her out of a bad dream. Casey waited expectantly for Gabbie to answer it, but the distant tapping of the typewriter didn't even pause. At the fourth ring, Casey rose to her feet and walked back into the house. The white phone was sitting on an end table, still intermittently ringing. She glanced toward the room where Gabbie was working. Perhaps Gabbie didn't want anyone to know she was here, Casey thought. But she couldn't ignore the ringing and finally answered it.

"Hello," a male voice responded cheerfully, sending Casey's heartbeat racing at triple speed. "Is that you, Gabbie?"

For a moment the rich timbre of the man's voice had reminded her of Flint. Her knees had nearly buckled beneath her as she sank onto the sofa adjoining the end table.

"No, no, it's not Gabbie." She had trouble finding her voice. "I'll get her for you."

She set the receiver down before the man could reply and hurried to the room where Gabbie was working. She tapped lightly on the open door.

"There's a phone call for you."

"Who is it?" Gabbie glanced up from her typewriter reluctantly.

"I didn't ask. It's a man."

"That's something." Gabbie smiled broadly, leaving her desk to enter the living room.

It was impossible for Casey not to listen to the one-sided conversation.

"Hello . . . I was working. You know how I am when I'm in front of that typewriter. It would take an explosion of dynamite beneath my chair . . . .Oh, that was Casey Gilmore. You remember Flint telling us about her. She's going to be staying with me until her father's out of the hospital . . . .I'm finishing up an article, so why don't we make it next weekend? That's a date, then. 'Bye now, love you."

Gabbie turned to Casey after replacing the receiver on the hook. Her eyes twinkled with laughter.

"You were right, it was a man," she said. "My dad. They're coming over next weekend. Mom and dad are both fishing addicts, so it's just about impossible to keep them away from Big Mac for long. Big Mac is the lake," Gabbie explained. "An affectionate abbreviation of Lake McConaughy used by the local people."

Casey's attempt at a smile barely lifted the corners of her mouth. She knew there was no chance that her father would be released from the hospital next week. His hip had to remain in traction another ten days. Wasn't it bad enough that she had to be staying with Flint's sister? Did she have to meet his parents, too?

If Gabbie noticed her lack of enthusiasm at the news, she didn't comment about it. She quickly excused herself and returned to the small den she used for her writing.

CHAPTER THIRTEEN

A SNAIL POWERED THE HANDS of the clock so that each day seemed to contain forty-eight hours for Casey. Forty-eight hours in which the full futility of her love hung like a yoke around her shoulders, weighting her down until she felt that she could stand it no longer. Gabbie had done her best in the last four days to fill in Casey's hours. She worked only in the mornings and devoted the rest of her time to planning activities for herself and Casey.

Two afternoons she had driven Casey to Scottsbluff in her little sports car so that Casey could see her father. But those were strenuous, tension-filled hours during which Casey had to watch every word she spoke lest she should give away the true state of her emotions. Her father had improved considerably and was looking forward to returning home. For the first time Casey even had difficulty discussing the affairs of the ranch with her father. It seemed that all their sentences contained the word Flint. Now even that life was linked solidly with him.

The ever-perceptive Gabbie realized the problem and immediately set about rectifying the situa-

tion. The following afternoons she conducted
Casey on a sightseeing tour of Ogallala which was
just ten miles from Lake McConaughy. The man-
sion on the hill, Front Street, Boot Hill Cemetery,
all the attractions that made Ogallala the "Cowboy
Capital of Nebraska" were paraded before Casey.
But the faded museum pictures of cowboys at the
end of a long cattle drive had merely served up
images of Flint as Casey had so often seen him sil-
houetted against the sky, his farseeing eyes scan-
ning the horizon. The loneliness of Boot Hill
Cemetery struck a chord in the loneliness of her
own heart.

Gabbie then took her shopping, thrusting outfit
after outfit at her and insisting each would cheer
Casey up. Some of the more brightly colored ones
Casey had succumbed to, knowing that the gay
colors did much to emphasize her own attractiveness. So she bought the gay, sophisticated clothes,
trying to don a new image at the same time, only
to wonder afterwards why she had bothered.
Brightly colored cloth couldn't penetrate her heart
and brighten its dulling ache.

Just being with Gabbie had strengthened
Casey's determination to fight this torment. The
only trouble was, it was a major war. The battle
came every time Flint's image drifted before her
eyes. Restless and edgy, Casey found her only
release in constant activity. That way she could
tumble into bed at nights and be assured her

exhaustion would bring instant sleep. But the heavy dreamless sleep, while it kept away the nightmares, always ended early in the morning and, just as this morning, a long day stretched mockingly out, daring her to fill it without Flint.

Was it the breeze through the cottonwood trees or herself that had just sighed so heavily, Casey wondered. Sometimes the two sounds blended so well that it seemed the earth was mourning with her. Her wristwatch said it was nearly nine o'clock, but the sun had already driven away the coolness of the night. Casey's walk along the beachfront had already taken her out of sight of the lake cabin where Gabbie was working. She climbed up on a rock and gazed out across the lake at the scattering of boats. She removed a cigarette from its pack in her beach bag and inexpertly lit it. Smoking was a newly acquired habit of Casey's. While it did give her something to do with her hands, it brought no relaxation for her, only a burning in her throat.

She sat motionless on the rock, letting the heat of the sun burn her legs, bare below the scanty brief of her bikini. It was strange how physical inactivity would immediately give her mind an opportunity to bring back memories of Flint. The warmth of the sun on her skin rekindled the fire of his embrace while the gentle stirrings of the wind caressed her. She had only to close her eyes and feel his breath upon her face as he rained kisses on her. The tremor such memories caused was more painful and violent than the earthquakes of the initial happenings.

"It isn't fair!" she moaned, rising quickly to her feet.

All of nature was conniving against her. Even the shadowy gray clouds on the horizon reminded her of the color of his eyes—a gray that could shift from the burnished brightness of old silver to the violent, turbulent shade of storm clouds and on to the metallic hardness of iron and steel.

Casey paused briefly near the water's edge. She kicked off her sandals, shrugged off the terrycloth beach jacket, removed her wristwatch and piled them with her beach bag and towel before wading into the water. The coolness felt refreshing against the heat of her skin. In minutes she was cleaving through the water with the rhythmic strokes of the Australian crawl. Driving herself as if she could race away from the torment that clung tenaciously at her heels, she struck out farther and farther, again using physical exertion to overcome the virulent memories. One, two, three, four strokes, then head out of the water to expel the air in her lungs and take another breath. Through the pounding of the blood in her head and the splashing of water from her own movements, she dimly heard a voice call out. For a split second it registered as being nearby, although she didn't recall seeing any other swimmers on the beach. Then her outstretching hand encountered a solid wall in front of her. Her momentum carried her into it, a glancing blow striking the side of her head with startling pain. Water washed over the top of her as she struggled to regain the surface, fighting the pain that was hammering away at her skull.

A hand suddenly grabbed hold of one of her arms, then another. Suddenly she was hauled out of the water to lie gasping on the deck of a small sailboat. Red and gold sails hung limply above her head as she shook the water from her hair and tried to focus her eyes through the glimmering of water on her lashes.

"Are you all right?" A figure was bending over her. She blinked and wiped her eyes. "I called out to you, but you didn't hear me. The breeze died on me and she... the boat wouldn't answer to the rudder."

Casey pushed herself into a sitting position, a slight dizziness preventing her from doing any more.

"I'm okay. A little shaky, that's all." Her voice was tremulous, though she added a small smile to reassure the young man hovering so earnestly beside her. He smiled back at the news.

"I have some coffee in the thermos. You'd better have a cup." He walked carefully to the rear of the boat where there was a wicker basket.

Casey took the opportunity to study her assailant turned rescuer. He wasn't much older than herself, twenty-two or three perhaps. If he stood up straight, he'd probably be about six feet tall, she decided. His hair had been bleached almost white by the sun and was cut in a long shaggy style. His skin, what was visible through his sky-blue windbreaker and below his black swimming trunks, was an unbelievable shade of mahogany tan. When he turned back to her, she saw his eyes were a brilliant shade of blue. Ironically, what really registered with Casey was not his attractiveness, although she had noted it, but his complete lack of any resemblance to Flint. In fact, he was in complete contrast to him.

White teeth shone out at her as he handed her the red plastic cup steaming with hot coffee. He waited expectantly while Casey sipped it carefully, the hot liquid chasing off some of the chills.

"Thanks," she said, smiling gratefully up at him. "It's good."

"You didn't hit your head very hard, did you? You don't have a slight concussion or anything like that, I hope?" His blue eyes chased over her face and hair as if he could find some outward evidence of his fear.

"I really don't know." She laughed a little nervously, her hand reaching up to touch the tender spot under her hair. There was no doubt it was sore, but Casey was sure it was only a bump. "I don't think so. Just bruised."

"That's a relief." There was a smiling sigh and shake of his head. He extended a brown hand to her from his kneeling position. "My name is Sean, Sean Sorenson. It was so nice bumping into you, Miss—"

"Casey Gilmore."

The red and gold sails stirred, then billowed out as the wind filled them. Sean was instantly bustling with activity, grabbing a rope and the handle of the rudder. Casey, who had never been aboard a sailboat before, watched him with interest. Soon the boat was skimming along the surface of the water.

"How about a ride around the lake . . . as sort of compensation for the knock on the head," Sean called out.

Casey hesitated. She didn't really know him, even though she did like him. He hardly seemed the sinister type, but one never really knew.

"I promise I won't spirit you away," he added during her hesitation. A teasing sparkle lit his eyes. "And I'll stay close to the shoreline so that if I get fresh you can hop over the side and swim to the beach."

Casey laughed then. "I'd love a sail under those circumstances. I've never been on one before. It always looked like fun, though."

"You have a treat in store for you," Sean promised, his attention on the sails and the tugging rope.

And Casey did. The boat glided effortlessly through the waters as silently and as gracefully as a swan. Keeping true to his word, Sean guided it along the shore. Casey felt she was being spirited along by a magic carpet, so silent was their journey without the obtrusive noise of a motor. Rocky fingers jutted out into the lake, each sandstone and rock formation unique and rugged and wildly beautiful. The long stretches of beaches gleamed whitely while the water that lapped at their edges reflected the brilliant blue of the sky. Brightly colored swimsuits and summer wear dotted the land where tourists and vacationers enjoyed this paradise of sun and beach that resembled an oasis in the middle of the plains. It was all terribly exhilarating to Casey. She told herself that she had almost forgotten Flint, even though the very thought reminded her of him again. There was a barely formed wish that he could be here with her now. The snowy-white petals of a prickle poppy plant that was perched on the top of a jutting mesa like a lighthouse laughed out at her so that she didn't hear Sean question her.

"Hey, Casey!" he called again.

She turned, blinking at the veil of mist covering her eyes. Determinedly she blinked them away, waving to him that she heard him above the crack of the canvas.

"There's a marina in the next cove that has a pretty good restaurant. Do you feel like a sandwich?" Sean offered.

She smiled her agreement, adding a short

affirmative nod. She turned back toward the lake ahead of them so she wouldn't have to speak. Minutes later he was maneuvering the boat to the dock, efficiently and expertly guiding it until he leaped onto the wooden dock and secured the boat. Casey took his hand as he pulled her up to join him.

"Wait a minute," he said, hopping back into the boat where he removed his windbreaker and replaced it with a yellow shirt. He tossed the blue jacket to Casey.

"You wear it—and these too." Sean tossed a pair of thonged sandals onto the wooden dock. "They'll be too large, but 'No shirt, no shoes, no service' is the local motto around here."

The lightweight jacket complemented the vivid blue and gold of her new bikini. The ends of the sleeves had elastic bands so that Casey could push the material to her elbows. They both laughed as Casey clomped along the dock in the oversize sandals. It was hard to keep from walking out of them. But it was shared laughter, without any mocking or jeering overtones.

In the restaurant Casey settled for a hamburger and soft drink while Sean ordered a more hefty assortment. Her appetite had been non-existent for the last few days, so it surprised her when she was able to down the hamburger with little difficulty. Conversation with Sean, a comparative stranger, was remarkably easy. It was all light and nonsensical, not touching on any subject to any great depth. Casey did learn that he was a student at Creighton University in Omaha, working in Ogallala for the summer.

"I work at one of the resorts down the beach, servicing boats, etcetera," he said. "And on my day off, I always take a busman's holiday. Sailing is my one great love, next to medicine. What about you? Do you live here, work here, or just on holiday?"

Casey smiled grimly. "My family has a ranch up north in the Sand Hills. My dad broke his hip this spring when he was thrown from a horse and he's in the hospital in Scottsbluff. He hired a man to take his place. So, since mom was in Scottsbluff with dad, I was obliged to stay here in Ogallala as opposed to remaining on the ranch alone with a bachelor."

"Sounds terribly Victorian." Sean laughed. "Who are you staying with here?"

Casey hesitated, sipping her Coke through a straw. "Gabrielle McCallister. She's the sister of the man we hired."

"McCallister!" Sean whistled, studying Casey with new eyes. "That's high-priced help, if you're referring to the local cattle baron family."

Her neck stiffened slightly. She didn't like the conversation and wished now that she hadn't responded to his question, or at least not truthfully. Then Casey checked her rising temper. Sean certainly didn't mean anything personal by his comment and she was being childish again.

"My father wanted the best," she said finally.

"From all I've heard, he got it," Sean's eyes widened as he nodded his head in affirmation.

"What time is it getting to be?" Casey moved restlessly in her chair. "Gabbie will be expecting me pretty soon."

Sean glanced at his bare arm, then up to the clock above the restaurant door. "Quarter to one."

Casey stared at the clock in amazement. The sailboat ride hadn't seemed to take any time at all. She had always been back from the beach by noon. She knew for sure that Gabbie would be worried about her. She turned quickly back to Sean.

"Do you mind? I'd really like to leave now. I didn't realize it was so late." Casey rose from her chair to add emphasis to her request.

"No, not at all." Sean rose from his own chair, reaching in the pocket of his shirt for his money.

They had come far along the coast from where Casey had met Sean. The sun had reached its zenith and hovered there glaring down at them unmercifully. The lake was a sheet of glass, shimmering back with the brilliant rays of the sun. What little breeze that had been stirring was practically a light breath now. Casey longed to hurry, but Sean was already paddling to aid the teasing wind that occasionally tickled the sails. At last she spotted the tumble of rocks near a cluster of cottonwoods where she had left her belongings. Sean obligingly beached the boat a short distance away on a more sandy area of the beach.

"I really enjoyed the sail," said Casey, trying to express her sincerity even though she was in a terrible hurry. She removed his jacket and handed it back to him. "And the lunch, too."

"I'd like to see you again, Casey." His blue eyes roamed over her face in admiration.

It had been a pleasant interlude, but Casey wasn't sure she wanted to repeat it. "I don't know how long I'll be here," she stalled.

"I'll probably see you out swimming again. We'll make a date, okay?" Sean suggested hopefully.

"Okay," she agreed nervously. "I really had better get going. I'll see you soon, I'm sure, Sean."

Casey helped him push the boat off the sandy bottom and remained long enough on the beach to wave a polite goodbye before scurrying toward the place she had left her things. But when she got there, they weren't there. Casey couldn't believe it. She looked around at the landmarks. She was sure it was the same place. Of course, she had been gone long enough for them to have been stolen. Disgustedly she set off for the cabin, cursing her own stupidity for leaving them out in plain view for anyone to see.

As Casey drew even with the cottonwoods, there

was a rustling of twigs and grass, followed by the crunching of rocks. She glanced apprehensively at the shadowy place, then stopped abruptly in her place as a tall, lean figure stepped out. It was as if an electric shock went through her as her hand crept to her chest to still the erratic hammering of her heart.

CHAPTER FOURTEEN

"WERE YOU LOOKING for these?" Eyes as gray and cold as the shadowy clefts of an iceberg glared at Casey as Flint extended his hand which held the missing beach items. He wasn't an apparition. He was really standing there in front of her.

"How . . . how did you get here?" Breathlessly she drew her scattered thoughts together and tried to still the trembling in her voice. "What are you doing here?"

"Keeping track of irresponsible females!" he spat out angrily.

An engulfing wave of heat saturated her skin as his gaze raked over her scanty attire. The exposure of so much of her bare flesh had never bothered her until now when he made her feel so cheap and indecent. Her hand moved involuntarily to cover the vee of her top.

"Put this on," Flint ordered, tossing the ochre gold robe to her.

Casey shrugged into it willingly, clutching the front together tightly. At least her skin didn't burn from his glance. Her eyes were held captive by his until the very intensity of his gaze forced her to look away.

"I'd better get back to the cabin," Casey murmured, turning away from him toward the cabin. "Gabbie will be getting worried."

"Worried!" Flint covered the distance between them before Casey could even begin to move away. He grabbed her shoulders and shook her violently, unmoved by her wide frightened eyes. "You idiotic female! What do you think I'm here for? Gabbie's half out of her mind from worry!"

"You're . . . you're hurting me!" Casey gasped, her teeth nearly rattling out of her head, even while her senses were keenly tuned to his touch.

"I'd like to do a lot more than that!" The shaking stopped, but she remained firmly in his grip. His eyes bored into her. "When I think of what you've put Gabbie through, I could cheerfully throttle you."

Casey tried to push away from him, but he jerked her nearer. She was fighting more than the hands biting into her shoulders. She was fighting the desire to be in his arms, to turn her face up to his and invoke the physical response she knew she was capable of creating. All she wanted to do was put her arms around him and have him hold her and never let her go. She swallowed hard to gain control, to force her body to obey her mind and not her heart.

"I know I'm late," Casey asserted calmly, "It was unavoidable. The wind died down and there wasn't enough breeze for the sails. Sean had to paddle most of the way back and it really took a long time."

"Oh, Sean did, did he? How gallant," Flint sneered, his contemptuous gaze causing more pain. "That's just about as convenient as running out of gas, isn't it?"

Her temper exploded with white-hot intensity as her hand lashed out and connected with his cheek. The stinging of her hand didn't really tell her what she had done. It was the red mark on Flint's cheek that showed her. His reaction was just as swift. Before she could struggle, he had both of her hands pinned behind her back at the same time that he lifted her off her feet and carried her to the trunk of a fallen tree. Effortlessly he pushed her over his knee, ignoring her kicking feet, and began paddling her rear end with hard, stinging slaps. Her cries of pain and anger went unheeded. At last he released her, standing her on the ground and studying the trickle of angry tears down her face. Casey couldn't avoid rubbing the injured portion of her body even as she stared up at him angrily.

"Do you want to try that again?" Flint stood in front of her, his hands on his hips, the bold light of challenge in his eyes. "Because if you do, I'll be happy to oblige you again."

"I hate you." Her voice was incredibly husky. "I hate you!"

"Is that supposed to surprise me?" he mocked.

"I don't particularly care!" Her brown eyes

snapped fiercely at him. "I'm tired of you constantly treating me like a child. I'm twenty-one. All I want you to do is stay out of my life." It was impossible to ask him to stay out of her heart.

"I'm looking forward to the day I can wash my hands of you, don't worry. Right now all I want to do is deliver you safely back to Gabbie." Flint reached out and grasped her wrist, dragging her behind him through the trees where the chrome of his car winked through the leaves.

He shoved her into the front seat, tossing her belongings in after her, and then climbed behind the wheel himself. He glanced at her once as if to make sure she wasn't trying to escape. Casey sat stiffly against the door, determinedly keeping her gaze riveted to the outside. The pain in the lower portion of her body was hard to ignore, especially with the heat of the sun warming the upholstery of the seat. Flint inserted the keys in the ignition, then paused before starting the motor. She could feel his eyes on her, but she refused to meet them.

"Casey, I want you to promise me something," Flint stated grimly.

She turned her belligerent brown eyes on him. "Don't you get tired of bossing people around?"

"I want you to promise that you will never go off like that again without telling Gabbie where you're going." Flint completely ignored her gibe, although his eyes did narrow a trifle menacingly.

"Why don't you make it an order?" A bittersweet smile matched the glare in her eyes. "After all, you are the big boss man." She spat out the words.

"We could trade insults all day," Flint drawled. He was trying to keep his temper under control and Casey was trying desperately to rile him. "All I want from you is your word that you won't send Gabbie off on another wild goose chase like this, worrying herself sick since nine o'clock this morning. I'm asking for her sake, not my own."

"This morning?" Casey echoed. A frown creased her forehead. "Why should she be looking for me then? I never come back from the beach until around noon. She always works in the morning."

"Because I called this morning and wanted to talk to you. Why I called is immaterial right now. She went down to the beach to look for you and couldn't find a trace, except for your things lying on the sand. The natural assumption was that you went swimming. And since she couldn't see you in the water, she was afraid you'd drowned. Thank goodness Gabbie isn't the type to panic. Instead of calling the rescue unit and have them drag the lake for your body, she called me and saved us a lot of embarrassment since you were out all morning with your Scandinavian boyfriend."

"He's not my boyfriend." Casey retorted savagely, still stunned by the news that she had been the object of a search since nine o'clock that morning.

"It's none of my business what he is," Flint

answered just as sharply, "whether he's your cousin, boyfriend or lover!"

He didn't give her an opportunity to reply, immediately turning the ignition and gunning the motor so that any words Casey might have wanted to say would have been drowned out by the noise. She bit her lip tightly to keep the tears back until the taste of blood in her mouth made her aware of what she was doing. But she knew she would have preferred Gabbie calling the rescue squad and enduring that and the explanations that followed, rather than face this inquisition with Flint.

Gabbie was on the veranda when they returned, her bright, blue green eyes taking in the tension between the two. If Casey had been less wrapped up in her own emotions, she might have noted that there was a remarkable lack of anxiety on Gabbie's face.

"Casey, are you all right?" Gabbie rushed forward to embrace her lightly. "You gave us a terrible scare. Where were you?"

"I went sailing," Casey inserted before Flint could put in a sarcastic remark she was sure was waiting on the edge of his tongue. "I'm afraid I didn't keep track of the time."

"No doubt she was too enthralled with the company she was keeping." Flint glared at her briefly.

"Company?" Gabbie echoed, looking to Casey for an explanation.

Casey gritted her teeth and explained, aware of

the piercing gaze of the gray eyes. "I met this boy who works at one of the resorts here. He offered to take me sailing and I accepted."

An incredibly uncomfortable silence followed her words. The crushing lack of sound seemed to have been ordered by Flint so that the full foolishness of her actions could sink in.

"Gabbie, get us something cold to drink." Flint's gaze never strayed from Casey as he barked out his command.

Gabbie raised a dark eyebrow at Casey before gliding quietly off the veranda. The heat of the afternoon sun suddenly became oppressive, and Casey found the atmosphere on the veranda unbearably stifling. She moved closer to the railing, gazing out to the lake and the promise of cool refreshing water. She glanced hesitantly back at Flint, her stomach unwillingly turning over at the very sight of his tanned face and auburn-tinted hair.

"What do you mean 'you met this boy'?" he asked ominously.

"Just what I said." She turned her back to him and leaned her hands against the wooden railing around the veranda. Her fingers gripped the boards until her knuckles were white.

"When did you meet him?" Flint continued his cross-examination. The sudden racing of her heart indicated that he was moving closer and the shadow on the board floor confirmed it.

"Today," she replied in a light and deliberately uncaring voice.

"Do you mean you met some stranger today and went sailing with him?" There was no mistaking the anger in his voice. An invisible hand wrapped itself around her heart and squeezed until Casey wanted to cry out from the pain. "You let a complete stranger pick you up! You can't be that naive?"

"Stop making a federal case out of it!" Casey lashed out. His criticism of her was unbearable. He would never believe how supremely innocent the morning had been. "Sean was a very nice young man who had nothing more on his mind than sharing a boat ride."

Flint spun her around, pushing her beach robe over her shoulders until it pinned her arms at her sides like a straitjacket. Her brief bikini was exposed to his censorious gaze. "With you dressed like that, he just thought about a boat ride. Oh, he thought about a ride all right, but not that kind!"

"What's the matter?" Casey taunted, fire darting out of her brown eyes as she stared defiantly into his. "Are you regretting not seducing me when you had the chance?"

She could feel the incredible tenseness in his body transferring itself from his grip on her shoulders to her. His gaze fastened on her trembling lips and a coursing flood of heat raced through her body. Her lips parted in anticipation of his kiss,

wanting, desiring it with every part of her body.
She could see the answering flash of desire in his
eyes. Flint had started to draw her toward him
when the screen door from the house to the
veranda slid open.

"Whoops! Bad timing. I'll go get some cookies,"
Gabbie called gaily at the sight of the couple. She
turned around swiftly to go back into the house.

"Don't bother," Flint said, releasing Casey and
walking swiftly toward the umbrella-topped table.
"You didn't interrupt a thing."

"My mistake." Gabbie smiled widely. "I thought
I had."

Casey joined them a little more slowly, needing
time to gain control of herself and her emotions.
The silence at the table could have been cut with a
knife and served in generous portions. Her hand
trembled too badly to hold a glass, so she sat very
still in her chair and studied a loose thread on the
sleeve of her robe. The scraping of Flint's chair
brought her tear-bright gaze upward. She was
imprisoned by the tired, defeated look on his face.
For a moment, she could have sworn that his eyes
were pleading with her and she swallowed convul-
sively. But just as quickly, they hardened into steel,
austere and inflexible.

"I have to get back to the ranch," Flint uttered
harshly. "Do you have enough manners to walk
me to the car, Casey?"

Somehow she managed to stand on her weak

legs while Gabbie murmured that she would take care of the cleaning up. How she wished Gabbie would have gone with her. Then Flint wouldn't have been able to subject her to any more of his barbed remarks. Flint waited with cold politeness for Casey to precede him. Her composure was stiff and unnatural and the irritated expression on his face told her he noticed it. "I'm sorry you made this trip needlessly," Casey said once they reached the pickup truck. "I wish I could have made it worthwhile for you by drowning."

"Even if you were dead," Flint sighed heavily, his gaze roaming over her intense face, "I believe you'd come back to haunt me." He opened the door and crawled into the cab, then stared at her with disconcerting blandness. "It's useless to suggest that you shouldn't see that boy again, I suppose."

"Yes," Casey answered calmly, because she had no intention or desire to see Sean again.

"I don't think you plan to see him again." One corner of his mouth lifted with mocking amusement as he studied her face. "But you wouldn't want to give me the satisfaction of knowing that."

Damn his perception, Casey cursed silently while she cocked her head to one side in a gesture of defiance. "I might have a date with him tonight for all you know."

"You might." Flint's mouth twitched and his eyes glittered humorously. "But somehow I just don't think you do."

"I've walked you to your truck, Mr. McCallister. It's time you left." His total sureness that he was right irked her beyond words.

"You're still the same innocent prickle poppy trying to lodge your thorns into anybody who comes too close to you, aren't you, Casey?" Flint mocked, starting the motor and reversing the gears.

"Only when it's the wrong person." She turned on her heel and retreated toward the cabin, the sound of the truck's tires moving over gravel, interspersed with muted laughter from the driver, following her.

CHAPTER FIFTEEN

"AND THIS IS MY FATHER, Lucas McCallister." Gabbie wrapped her arm affectionately around the tall man who bore such an uncanny resemblance to Flint.

Casey had difficulty looking into the light gray eyes so similar to Flint's when he was in a teasing mood. The incredibly charming smile was the same, one corner of his mouth lifting higher than the other, but his father's hair was a darker shade of brown, almost black, with a very distinguishing touch of gray at the temples. He was still an imposing figure of a man who was considerably attractive for his advanced years.

"How do you do, Casey Gilmore." His hand clasped hers warmly, the resonant timbre of his voice chasing away some of her nervousness. She gazed hesitantly into his eyes, basking in the warm glow that looked back. "We've been looking forward to meeting you."

Lucas McCallister glanced affectionately at the slender, auburn-haired woman at his side. Jade green eyes smiled welcomingly at Casey, enhanced strangely by the laughter lines that edged them. She couldn't help smiling back at them.

"We've heard so much about you, Casey, that you seem part of the family." The older woman's smile was genuine. It lifted some of the dread that Casey had been feeling.

"That's very kind of you, Mrs. McCallister," Casey returned.

In the last few days she had been hoping that Flint's parents would be cold, snobbish people so that her love for him wouldn't extend to them. Now that she had actually met them, their open-armed friendliness was shattering that hopeful illusion. Except they were drawing her into the circle of their love.

"Call me Meg," Flint's mother insisted, squeezing Casey's hand affectionately. "We're hardly a formal family."

"You two run along out to the veranda. Casey and I will bring the lemonade and glasses," Gabbie ordered, flashing a proud smile toward Casey.

She had to assure her mother that she didn't need her help before the pair finally made their exit, leaving Gabbie alone with Casey. She turned her radiant face towards her.

"I'm terribly prejudiced, but I think I've got the greatest parents."

"They seem very youthful and fun," Casey acknowledged, staring after the retreating pair. Their warmth reminded her of her own family which she was beginning to miss.

Gabbie sighed, her eyes rounding as she fol-

lowed Casey's gaze. "My father could turn the
heart of any woman. Is it any wonder with four
brothers and a father that looks like that the men I
meet seldom measure up? I'll probably be doomed
to spinsterhood."

"I doubt that," Casey laughed, looking back at
the attractive dark-haired girl.

But from Casey's point of view it wasn't a laugh-
able observation. Not when she was faced with a
future of comparing the men she might meet with
Flint. She had the terribly empty feeling that she
was one of those women who only loved once in
their lifetime. And for her, that love was Flint.
Only she wasn't destined to possess his love—a
knowledge that didn't make the future look too
happy.

She accepted the tray of glasses Gabbie handed
her and started toward the outdoor veranda. As
she passed the mirror in the living room, Casey
was surprised by the composed reflection that
looked back at her. The haltered sundress she was
wearing was a vivid red that cast a rosy glow to her
cheeks. Only a bit of the torment, she felt, was visible in the haunted shadow of her eyes. Otherwise
she looked like any other normal healthy girl of
her age.

"How's your father?" Lucas McCallister
inquired when Casey entered the veranda and
placed the tray she was carrying on the table where
he was seated.

"He's much better. Just beginning to champ at the bit to get back to the ranch," Casey replied.

"A very good sign in a rancher," he chuckled.

"Which usually means they should stay in bed for at least another week," Meg inserted with a knowing gleam in her eye when she looked at her husband and then back to Casey.

"My mother would agree with you," Casey laughed, "but then I'm a bit like Dad—anxious to get things back to the status quo." A fervent wish that Casey knew secretly would never come true.

"Of course, it will be some time before your father can get around like he used to. He'll have to be content to do some armchair managing for a while." Gray eyes twinkled at her. "But then my son has told me of your assertion that you could run the ranch quite adequately."

"Women's work isn't restricted to the household anymore." The sharpness in her voice was more for the absent Flint than for his father.

"Still, it's a heavy responsibility for a slip of a girl," Lucas smiled, glancing at his wife. "Country gals are pretty tough, but there's nothing wrong in having a man around that you can lean on when the occasion warrants it." He winked boldy at Casey. "And even when it doesn't." Casey's cheeks flamed red hot as the teasing voice subtly linked her with Flint. "How are things at the ranch?"

"I really don't know," she answered haltingly.

"Oh? I understood Flint was here to see you this

week." His head tilted inquiringly toward her. "I presume he came to discuss business. Perhaps it was of a more personal nature?"

"It . . . it . . . w-was rather strange circumstances that brought him here," Casey stammered. "Besides, he usually talks everything over with my father."

"Yes, he probably would. No offense, Casey, but I can't really see my son reporting to a woman, even a liberated one," he chuckled.

"Flint has told us so much about your family that Luke and I are really looking forward to meeting them sometime." Meg McCallister changed the subject easily, drawing Casey's attention away from the older version of Flint.

Casey took the opportunity, now that the initial shock of meeting someone who looked so much like Flint had worn away, to study his mother. Her auburn hair was a shade redder than Flint's, even though it was elegantly peppered with gray, and when she smiled as she was doing now, there were two youthful dimples in her cheeks.

"Did you know that it was only after Flint met your father that he decided to take the job?" Meg asked. "Flint respects him a great deal."

"I know dad thinks a lot of him, too," Casey admitted. "Just knowing he had someone as experienced and competent as Flint made it easier for dad to accept the fact that he would have to stay in the hospital. It eased mother's mind, too, knowing there was a man in charge."

"You have a very rare trait, Casey." A voice spoke from behind her. "Praising a man behind his back and damning him to his face. Very unusual."

The blood washed out of her face at the sound of the voice. She nearly tipped the pitcher of lemonade over as she spun in her chair to face it. Flint stood directly behind her, looking down at her with a peculiarly pleased smile on his face. She wanted to run, to hide, but she was hypnotized by Flint's mocking gaze.

"I brought Mark along with me, but I think he went down to inspect the beach. He's a remarkable expert on the different kinds of fish that are found in the lake." His eyes released her as he turned to his parents. "Mom, dad, all set for a weekend on the water?"

"I plan to catch my limit." Lucas rose and took his son's hand. "You caught us all by surprise. We didn't expect to see you." Lucas cast the still slightly dazed Casey a compassionate glance. Flint followed it.

"Don't mind her. She's usually this overjoyed to see me," he said as he turned toward his mother. "My ears have been burning for the last thirty miles. You must have been talking about me."

"What a conceited male ego!" Gabbie exclaimed, handing Flint a frosty glass of lemonade and pushing him into a nearby chair.

"You were only discussed indirectly." Meg included Casey in her smile which Casey found hard put to return. "We were actually getting to know Casey, so if your name was mentioned, it was inadvertent."

"What I'd like to know, Flint, is why you never told us what a charming lady Casey was?" Lucas demanded, leaning closer to his son. "I always thought you had quite a good eye for beauty."

Casey's face was suffused with color. She didn't know how much more of this family matchmaking she could take, especially with Flint regarding her reactions with so much interest. It wasn't any consolation telling herself it was only good-natured teasing. And it was very apparent that no one was going to come to her rescue. But of course, they couldn't know the pain their innocent teasing caused. Flint was taking such delight in her discomfort.

"Hey, sis!" Mark bounded onto the veranda, his face wreathed in a smile. "This is really a super place! Boy, I wish I could have spent a week here. You can take my place on the ranch any time."

Casey rose quickly to greet him, fighting off the desire to cling to him as if he were a life preserver. He was just too grown up for any affectionate greetings. Just standing beside him gave her extra courage when Flint spoke up to introduce Mark to his parents.

"I've heard the fishing is terrific here," said Mark after Flint mentioned that his parents were here for that purpose. "They've had some record-

size catches, haven't they? I've heard people fly in
from Texas just to fish here."

Lucas McCallister was quick to take up the
change of conversation, which Casey was eternally
thankful for. It gave her a chance to check her
clamoring heart while Flint and his father regaled
Mark with tales of fish that got away. It was exqui-
sitely sweet torment to study Flint unobserved, to
mark in her memory forever the leanness of his
cheeks, the dark lashes that lazily veiled his eyes,
and his brown hair that caught a hint of the sun's
fire. But when her gaze strayed to the sensual curve
of his mouth, shivers raced down her spine, leaving
a burning trail of fire that spread throughout her
body. The yearning to feel those lips on hers again
was overpowering. Stripped of all her defenses and
conscious of only one person, Casey nearly leaped
from her chair when a hand touched her arm.

"It's lunchtime," Gabbie spoke quietly, her blue
green eyes sympathizing with the agony mirrored
in Casey's. "Would you like to give me a hand?"

"Of course," Casey agreed, somehow avoiding
contact with Flint's gaze as it narrowed on her.

"I'm sorry I startled you." Gabbie touched her
arm comfortingly as they walked into the house.
"But your face is terribly transparent sometimes. I
didn't think you'd want Flint to see. Although I
would have, so I could tell him what an utter fool I
thought he was."

"Thank you," Casey murmured, knowing how

shamed she would have felt if Flint had looked up at her earlier and surprised that look of love that must have been on her face. "It's not his fault that he's not in love with me. It's just one of those things that happens or it doesn't."

"Some people get the measles, too, but they get over them a lot faster you know." The cynicism in Gabbie's voice was quite apparent and touching.

"You make it sound as if heartbreak lasts forever," Casey laughed weakly, trying to add a bit of lightness to the conversation that was threatening to bring tears to her eyes. But Gabbie just looked at her with a glance that plainly asked, "Doesn't it?"

Both of the girls were aware that it would do no good to discuss the situation any further. They were a silent and grim team, retrieving the tray of already prepared sandwiches from the refrigerator, and the salads and the chips. It only took two trips from the kitchen to the table on the veranda and practically everything had been carried out. Only a bowl of potato salad, the napkins and the silverware were left to be fetched. Casey was a trifle mystified when Mark offered to help her. He was not usually so concerned about giving assistance even when it was his stomach involved. She became even more puzzled when, once they were in the kitchen, he shuffled back and forth on his feet nervously.

"This isn't like you, Mark," she jested, "volunteering for women's work."

"I wanted to talk to you." His glance bounced off her face as he lowered his voice. "Mr. McCallister just offered to take me fishing and I didn't know if I'd get another chance to talk to you alone."

"What's the matter?" Casey asked, the confiding tone in his voice startling her. "You certainly are old enough not to ask my permission to go along."

"I don't mean that." His forehead creased in a very determined frown. "You'll be coming back to the ranch in another week and there's something I think you should know. I thought it would be better coming from family than from a stranger telling you."

Casey longed to urge him to tell her what he was talking about, but it was so obvious from his serious, adultlike voice that it was difficult for him to explain and it embarrassed him as well. Not in her wildest imagination could she think of anything so dire that it would concern Mark, and it certainly couldn't be anything to do with Flint.

"Since you've been gone, Smitty has been seeing Brenda Fairlie," Mark blurted out in a rush, his cheeks a brilliant shade of red. Casey nearly sighed with relief. "The day you left, he took her out. They went to some restaurant and she started putting on airs like she always does. Smitty told her off, but she must have liked the caveman technique because she nearly fell in his arms apologizing. They've been inseparable ever since. Now, there's even talk that she won't be going back to college this fall." Mark glanced at his sister to see how she was taking the news.

The tears in her eyes weren't for the loss of Smitty, but for the sudden attack of brotherly devotion Mark had just shown. She wanted to throw her arms around him and hug him tightly, but she knew she could never do that. He had no other option but to assume that those tears were for Smitty.

"Thank you for telling me." Her voice was husky, but her smile at him was quite sincere.

"Well, I knew you and Smitty were a pretty steady couple. And I thought . . . well, it'd be easier if you knew before . . . ."

"It is," she answered simply. Casey glanced around her quickly, her eyes coming to a stop on the large bowl on the counter. "Here, you take the potato salad and I'll bring the rest in a minute."

"If you like, I can tell them you had to wash the silverware or something. I mean, if you need time to—"

"I'll be right there, Mark. I'm fine really," she assured him.

Casey honestly thought she was. She even smiled at Mark as he walked out of the room. She told herself that she was glad for Smitty and Brenda as she leaned against the sink. Good old steady Smitty, her lips trembled and her eyes filled with tears. This time he wouldn't be there, not even as a friend, because Brenda would never understand. Not that Smitty probably would have comforted her anyway, she thought as a couple of tears trickled down her cheeks. He had warned her about Flint and would have been more apt to say "I told you so" than offer solace. Still, it was like removing another rock from the already shaky foundation of her life.

"Did Mark mention that he was going fishing with my father?"

Casey stiffened at Flint's voice, but she didn't turn around. "Yes, yes, he did."

"I thought we could drive up to visit your father." He was walking closer.

"Whatever you say." Her voice rang out harshly. She suddenly felt too tired emotionally to argue with him, so she busied her hands with the silverware spread on the counter top. "I'll be out just as soon as I get this silver gathered together."

His fingers gripped her chin and twisted her face up toward him. Casey summoned all her pride to stare defiantly into his iron-gray eyes. There was no way he could miss the trail of tears.

"I was eavesdropping," Flint stated unapologetically. "I didn't realize Smitty's defection would affect you this deeply."

"There's a lot of things about me and my feelings you don't know, Mr. McCallister." She pushed his unresisting hand from her chin, then wiped away the telltale marks on her face.

"Every time I think I'm beginning to understand you, you change colors like a chameleon." Irritation laced his words.

"First I was a prickle poppy, now I'm a chameleon." A brightly defiant gleam sparkled out of Casey's brown eyes. "You're not very consistent yourself!"

CHAPTER SIXTEEN

"HAVE YOU TALKED THIS OVER with Flint?" Lucille Gilmore inquired, her blue eyes studying the tension-filled face of her daughter.

"With Flint? What has he got to do with it? What business is it of his?" Casey cried. "If I can't stay at Aunt Jo's, then I'll stay in a motel. But I'm not going back there!"

After an almost endless ride with Flint from Ogallala to the hospital in Scottsbluff, Casey had reached breaking point. It didn't matter any more if what she was proposing was cowardly, a form of running away. She just knew that she couldn't make that long ride back to Gabbie's with Flint. The agony of being so close to him, of enduring the stilted conversations between them, was tortuous. That was why Casey had lost no time in persuading her mother to walk with her to the lobby where she made her painful plea.

"Darling, it's not a question of whether Aunt Jo has room for you. Of course she does." Lucille moved her arm around Casey's shoulders in comfort. "That was a stupid remark I made, too, asking if you'd told Flint. Under the circumstances, that would hardly be likely, would it?"

Her mother's face blurred slightly as Casey stared at her. Did she know how she felt about him? Could she possibly have guessed?

"Now what kind of mother would I be if I couldn't even guess when my daughter fell in love? Here—" she rummaged in her purse and withdrew a set of keys "—these are for Aunt Jo's car in the parking lot. I'll make some excuse to Flint and your father. You run along and we'll talk later."

"Oh, mother!" Casey hugged her tightly, clasping the keys to freedom in her hand. "Thank you," she whispered fervently.

Her mouth was pressed firmly shut as she disentangled herself from her mother's arms, but she managed to smile gratefully at her before she hurried down the hall to the hospital exit. The parking lot was full of cars from weekend visitors. Casey scanned the rows trying to locate the yellow sedan belonging to her aunt. Panic raced through her as she failed to find it. It had to be there! It just had to be there!

The next thing she knew she was being seized roughly by the shoulders and pushed toward the green station wagon that had brought her here. She had a fleeting glimpse of a yellow sedan in the next row of cars. Flint didn't waste time on politeness, but shoved Casey into the wagon on the driver's side. She grabbed for the opposite handle to yank it open.

"Don't waste your time. It's locked." But he

caught hold of her hand for insurance and managed to start the car and reverse it with his free hand.

"You let me out of this car!" Casey demanded, twisting and turning her wrist, trying to free it from his hold so she could escape to the yellow car.

Flint gave her a cold look before returning his stormy gaze to the road in front of him.

"I never thought you were one of those weak women who run off and hide when their feelings get hurt. Just because some wet-nosed kid—" He inhaled deeply, but didn't finish his sentence.

"You're hurting my arm!"

Casey made no attempt to mask the pain in her voice as she enunciated as sharp and as clear as she could. Flint glanced at her meaningfully.

"I'm not about to commit suicide by jumping out of the car when it's traveling as fast as this," Casey pointed out.

Flint slackened the speed and released Casey's hand. They were on a graveled road now with the town behind them. There was a scattering of houses, then the countryside spread out before them, isolated fields of irrigated crops amidst the rolling hills. Finally Flint ground the car to a halt on the shoulder. Casey riveted her gaze to a distant sandstone bluff, fighting the powerful pull as gray eyes ordered her to look at him.

"I know it was a terrible blow hearing about Smitty." His voice was low and controlled. "But it will pass, Casey. You just have to give yourself time."

"Spare me the platitudes," Casey groaned, her hands reaching up to cover her ears.

"Why do you huddle against the door like that? I'm only trying to help." His gentle entreaty brought a louder pounding of her heart and an increased trembling to her body. It was nearly impossible not to respond to his coaxing tone.

A hard, callused hand reached up and captured one of Casey's hands, not roughly as before, but tenderly as one would hold a frightened bird. It would have been so easy to draw it away that Casey left it there.

"You'll meet someone else who will mean just as much to you," he said softly.

This time she turned to meet the shadowed eyes. She stared into the face of the man she adored with all her heart. A cry broke from her lips. "No, no, I never will!"

Sparks from the fire in his eyes darted over her before Flint doused them. "Of course you will," he answered with fierce determination.

"You're . . . you're being very kind, Flint." She looked away, blinking hastily at the tears rushing to fill her eyes. "But . . . but it . . . it just doesn't help right now."

"Oh, God, Casey, please don't cry," Flint moaned, covering the small distance between them before Casey could protest and drawing her into his arms. "I can't stand to see you cry," he declared, burying his face in her hair as Casey struggled ineffectually against the firmness of his embrace.

"Please, please let me go!" It was a breathless plea, one that her mind demanded she make while the rest of her reveled in his nearness.

He laughed bitterly, moving away so he could look down on his helpless prisoner. "Gabbie told me today I was fifty kinds of a fool for treating you the way I do. What she doesn't know is it's the only way I can keep my hands off you." Casey couldn't stop the little gasping cry at his words. "Even now, knowing those tears on your cheeks are for another man," Flint stated gruffly, "all I want to do is make love to you." He stared at the tremulous smile on her lips. "Does that amuse you?"

"No," she whispered, her dark eyes glowing with the unbelievable happiness.

"It should."

Her fingers reached up to still his voice and remained trembling on the sensual male mouth. "Are ... are you saying you love me?" Casey murmured.

"If you want it in black and white, then yes, I love you!"

She caught her breath at the violence in his voice. Her eyes closed to savor the glory of this moment before she spoke in a shaky but happy voice. "It's only fair to tell you that . . . that these tears are for a man who I thought only considered me a prickle poppy."

His hand jerked her chin upward so he could stare into her face. "You mean Smitty isn't . . . ."

"I mean I love you, Flint McCallister." It was unbelievable that those calm, composed words came from her throbbing body.

There was a split second of utter stillness before Flint covered her parted lips with his, possessively taking all the love she was giving and returning it tenfold. The next moments were tempestuous, heat-filled ones that threatened to continue until Flint determinedly held her away.

"When I think of the hell you've put me through, I could wring that precious neck!" The husky vibration in his voice shot quivering goose bumps of excitement through Casey. "I couldn't believe you didn't love me, but you denied it so violently the day I took you to Gabbie's that I had to believe you. But I wanted so badly for you to know my family as well as I knew yours."

"I thought you wanted to be rid of me, that you had just used me to satisfy your physical desires and were afraid that I would expect you to . . . to . . ." Casey tried to explain.

"To marry you," Flint finished for her, smiling at the flush that filled her cheeks. "I decided to marry you that day when you apologized to me so prettily. And now I'm going to do that. We're going to be married just as soon as we can get the license." He paused, his eyes roving over her face possessively. "And the wedding gown as pure a white as the petals on the prickle poppy."

"I thought the bride was supposed to arrange the wedding," Casey laughed breathlessly, enthralled by the love beaming out of his gray eyes.

"Usually," Flint agreed, pulling her back toward him to sprinkle kisses along the throbbing cord of her neck, pausing long enough to whisper in her ear, "but I'm afraid you might take too long and I don't think I can wait."

Casey gasped at the desire in his voice as she turned her mouth to find his, managing to murmur, "You're the boss man!"

Janet Dailey
Americana

Janet Dailey's perennially popular Americana series continues with more exciting states!

Don't miss this romantic tour of America through fifty favorite Harlequin Presents novels, each one set in a different state, and researched by Janet and her husband, Bill.

A journey of a lifetime in one cherished collection.

May titles
#31 NEW MEXICO
Land of Enchantment

#33 NEW YORK
Beware of the Stranger

"I know that you
resent me, Casey."

Flint's voice was ominously quiet as he continued. "But I'm here to manage this ranch, and I have to stay and do the job."

"How unfortunate for both of us!" Casey exclaimed, her voice cracking slightly. "I suppose we'll just have to make the best of a bad situation."

"I suppose so," Flint drawled, his keen gaze narrowing quizzically as the smoldering anger in Casey's eyes sharpened into an expression of pain. "Or, you could always leave," he suggested.

"Never," Casey retorted sharply. "I just wish you would get out of my—life." She could never tell him that she really wanted him out of her heart!

JANET DAILEY AMERICANA